THE NIGHT
TOLKIEN DIED

THE NIGHT TOLKIEN DIED

NADIA WHEATLEY

A Mark Macleod Book
Random House Australia
an imprint of
Random House Australia Pty Ltd
20 Alfred Street, Milsons Point NSW 2061

Sydney New York Toronto
London Auckland Johannesburg
and agencies throughout the world

First published in 1994
Copyright © Nadia Wheatley 1994

All rights reserved. No part of this publication
may be reproduced, stored in a retrieval system,
or transmitted in any form or by any means,
electronic, mechanical, photocopying, recording
or otherwise, without the prior written permission
of the Publisher.

National Library of Australia
Cataloguing-in-Publication Data:
　Wheatley, Nadia, 1949- .
　The night Tolkien died.
ISBN 0 09 182946 1.
I. Title.
A823.3

Cover illustration by Chris O'Doherty, aka Reg Mombassa.
Typeset by Asset Typesetting Pty Ltd, Sydney.
Printed by Australian Print Group, Victoria.
Production by Vantage Graphics, Sydney.

CONTENTS

Land/scape 9

The Blast Furnace 48

The Prodigal 72

The Known Soldier 90

The Most Unforgettable Character
I Have Ever Met 95

Pastoral 131

Quicksand 141

Listening to Mondrian 158

Women's Business 184

Melting Point 207

The Convict Box 239

The Night Tolkien Died 260

Acknowledgements:

I would like to thank the National Parks Service — Victoria, Department of Conservation and Natural Resources for permission to quote from its brochures in the story 'Land/scape'.

In regard to the story 'Melting Point', I would like to thank Gig Ryan for help with the Latin and Petro Alexiou for translating the Greek.

Overall, my thanks go to my friends and colleagues Libby Gleeson and Jenny Pausacker, who read and commented on most of the stories as they were being written or revised. In particular, Jenny spent a long time discussing the politics of 'The Most Unforgettable Character'.

Finally, I would like to thank Chris O'Doherty for the great cover and Martina O'Doherty for her support.

The following stories have been previously published:
'The Blast Furnace', in *Landmarks*, ed. Nadia Wheatley, Turton and Chambers, 1991
'Quicksand', in *The Blue Dress*, ed. Libby Hathorn, Mammoth, 1991
'The Convict Box', in *Goodbye and Hello*, ed. Clodagh Corcoran and Margot Tyrrell, Viking, 1992

This book is for Ken

LAND/SCAPE

(i) Holding Pattern

'This is Captain Klein speaking. Unfortunately there is a bit of a queue here at Tullamarine today, so we are entering a holding pattern. Our estimated arrival time will now be 2.10 pm ... '

The rest of the passengers sighed, tapped their watches, ostentatiously took out again the company reports that they'd stowed in their briefcases. Ant grinned. A short reprieve.

Ant was dreading the thought of five days with his father: it would be the longest time they had spent together since Tony had gone. Ant had been in Year 5 then. He was in Year 10 now. Quite a different person, in many ways. It wasn't just a matter of pubic hair, deeper voice, pimples and the height problem (Ant was 199 centimetres, and rising), but internal changes, to the way the brain thought about things. At ten, Ant hadn't had opinions on matters like Land Rights, the Mabo decision, nuclear energy, woodchipping, American military involvement in the Gulf, school uniforms, the republic, compulsory enrolment in the cadets; now he did. And he knew that his father would have different opinions.

Tony was a barrister. A member of the Establishment. As witnessed by the school that he made Ant go to: one of the most famously conservative boys' private schools in the country. It produced footballers, cricketers, graziers, senior executives, lawyers, doctors, and politicians of the Liberal and National parties. It had produced Ant's father (Captain of the First XI; Dux of the School; Head Prefect; Barrister) and Ant's grandfather (Captain of the First XV; Sports Captain; Prefect; Judge). Ant had to sit beneath their names and achievements written in gold on the polished oak boards in the chapel every morning. Had to blush with shame every time the sports teachers said 'I would have expected better of *you*, Hindmarsh,' whenever he bowled a mullygrubber, set up a try for the opposing team, served double faults into the net for an entire tennis match, or (on one spectacular occasion) managed to capsize the eight when they were only half a metre from the finishing line in the Greater Public Schools Regatta.

Why? Ant always wondered. Sure, in a general way he could see why they expected sporting ability from him: he should have had the genes for it. But — given that he didn't — why keep on expecting him to be able to do it? When every time he failed?

It was the same with the other teachers. Ant was

bright enough to be in the A class, bright enough always to pass everything, even Maths and Chemistry. But he was always in the bottom half. Unlike Tony (his teachers told him), who had topped his year every year from Kindergarten to Leaving. 'I would have expected more of *you*, Hindmarsh,' his English/History/Maths/Chemistry/Physics and even Japanese teachers always said. It was the kind of school where staff stay on forever, so most of them could actually remember teaching Tony, and one old codger even claimed to have taught the judge. Ant wished he was stupid so he could get into the Special class: they did Art, Metalwork, Woodwork, Tech Drawing, Carving and Casting, Photography, Screen Printing and Excursions. Even more to the point, Ant wished he could go to the Creative Arts High School two suburbs down the train line from where he lived. But Mum said not to waste his breath even asking Tony about it. The school Ant went to was a family tradition, from which Tony wouldn't budge, Mum said.

'We have now been given the clearance from the air traffic controller...'

Ant sighed, stowed away his sketch book and pencils in his shoulder bag, which was bright yellow with the Koorie flag on it and the words 'Land is Life'.

He tapped at his watch. It was 2.14. Oh well. Look on

the bright side. Most of Day 1 was nearly over. Then there'd just be Day 2, Day 3, Day 4, and on Day 5 he'd be travelling back home again. After that there'd still be nine days of holidays left for him to do what he liked doing: pottering around by himself at home, drawing, painting, developing photos, mucking about with the graphics programs on his Macintosh, or simply lying on his bed for hours to recoup the energy that his growing body seemed to drain from him. Ant hated the sort of holiday in which you had to rush about and *do* things all the time.

There was a nasty jolt as the wheels touched ground, then a sort of shudder seemed to run through the body of the plane, and now they were taxiing towards the terminal and Ant's father.

(ii) In the Wilds

It was half past five when they arrived at Cape Otway. The map showed this as just about the southernmost bit of the mainland, the beginning of the Great Australian Bight. To the south, there was nothing between here and Antarctica, Tony reckoned.

Despite himself, Ant grinned. When he was a little kid they used to have a map of the world on the back of the toilet door, and whenever his father took him in there,

LAND/SCAPE

Ant would get him to point out the big white land at the bottom, with its magic first three letters that Ant himself could read. He and Tony used to pretend that Antarctica belonged to Ant, and even that one day they would go there.

Ant glanced at his father now, to see if he remembered, but Tony was just saying how, this far south in mid winter, it would be dark in half an hour. 'So we'd better get a move on with this tent,' he added in the kind of voice that adults use to make an order sound polite.

Sometimes Ant's mind would seem to click out of his body for a moment, and he would see himself and the scene he was in as if it were a picture that he was photographing. That happened now: into his mind came an image of two extremely tall thin people, trying to put up a tent in sandy scrubby country as a high wind kept pulling at the canvas and ballooning it out of their control.

Then Tony yelled something and Ant was back in the real picture.

Not that Ant could see all that much of the real picture, because now drizzle was drizzling down inside his specs, so he wasn't being very helpful as Tony kept yelling stuff like 'Hang on to that guy rope!' and 'Just pull on the fly!'

The fly?

As far as Ant knew, flies were either insects or things in trousers. He stood there gawping.

'Don't stand there gawping!' his father said.

It wasn't Ant's fault he'd never been camping before. His father should have taken him when he was a little kid. But Tony was always so busy working that Ant couldn't remember a holiday of any variety that he'd ever been on with his father; nor for that matter could he remember his father going off camping with a bunch of mates, as some men did.

So why this?

Ant had a terrible feeling that Tony wanted this to be one of those Father-and-Son trips that happen in American books and television shows: where out in the wilds amongst the grizzly bears and snowcapped mountains, Dad and Junior subsist on root beer and wienies while they discuss the Facts of Life, the Meaning of Life, or whatever. How else could you explain why his father was taking him camping for five days in the middle of winter in a place that was just about at the South Pole?

At last the tent was up, the gas lamp was burning. Tony had even managed to get a fire going (he'd been a Queen's Scout when he was Ant's age, he informed his son) and was grilling sausages.

Ant was standing uselessly in the rain, with the water running down the inside of his specs.

'Why don't you get the sleeping bags out of the car? Make up the beds?'

So Ant got the bags, crawled into the tent with them and spread them in two parallel lines, trying to leave as much room as possible between them. The thought of sleeping so close to his father was somehow embarrassing.

He needn't have worried. As Ant backed out of the tent and stood up, he tripped over the guy rope and onto the upright aluminium pole at the opening of the tent, which snapped as he went down with it and then pierced upwards, slashing a great hole through the fly sheet. Meanwhile, as Ant lay there swathed in canvas, the drizzle abruptly changed to a downpour so fierce that it was as if not buckets but bathtubs of water were being dumped from the sky. And by the time Tony had pulled Ant and the tent pole and the drenched bags out of the wreckage, the fire had gone out and the half-raw, half-charred sausages were cold and wet.

'How on earth did you manage that?' Tony snapped.

Ant said nothing. How could he explain disability to a man who had been a Queen's Scout, Head Prefect, Captain of Cricket and (obviously) possessor of 20/20 vision? How could he say that he simply was not able to see with the rain coming down inside his specs?

Ant, however, was able to see his father making an effort to control himself, not to lose his temper completely. In a strained voice, Tony added, 'Oh well, nothing for it but to pack up and head back to Apollo Bay and look for a motel, I guess. I just hope we can find a vacancy in one that's not too expensive.'

Again Ant said nothing. His father seemed to interpret this as some sort of challenge to his last statement. 'I'm not *made* of money, you know,' Tony said tersely.

Aren't you? Ant wondered as he stashed the two sodden sleeping bags in the boot of the car. Aren't you? Tony would have to be earning a packet. Ant and his mother were certainly well provided for — Mum didn't work, she did uni courses; and the fees must be astronomical at Ant's horrible school.

Tony sighed, and took the wet sleeping bags out again. Ant had just put them on top of his father's bag of dry clothes.

(iii) His Father's Footsteps

Day 2 at least had good weather. A still, bright winter's day. The ocean as they headed west along the coast road was a blue that Ant tried to find from the little palette of colour words that he held in the thesaurus of his brain.

Ultramarine, cobalt, Prussian, indigo, lapis lazuli, sapphire, turquoise, peacock ...

If he were painting it he would mix a big blob of Prussian blue with a fraction of lemon yellow and a slightly bigger dab of cobalt, then blend in white for tone and lightness. Making the colours was one of Ant's favourite bits of painting, more important to him sometimes than the images he got down. He hadn't brought his paints on the holiday — it was too messy to travel around with oil drying on canvas boards — but he did have his sketch pad and a bundle of 8B pencils in his Land Rights bag. Would he dare get them out? Wouldn't Tony think it — sissy somehow, or stupid, or just a sheer waste of time? Tony would no doubt prefer bushwalking, hiking, rock climbing, clambering up mountains, or plunging down caves into the bowels of the earth.

Ant was aware that the car had turned off the bitumen onto a sandy track leading through coastal scrub towards the sea. 'Thought we'd have a bit of a hike. Stretch our legs,' Tony said, right on cue.

Ant left his sketch pad down the bottom of his bag but did wear his camera around his neck as they set off along the bank of the wide river outlet that took them to a deserted stretch of beach between two rocky promontories.

He glanced at his father: cameras were respectable, weren't they? Not wimpy or anything? After all, he was a tourist ...

His father nodded towards the camera, as if trying to take an interest. 'What sort is it?'

Here we go, Ant thought. Difference-of-opinion time. 'A Zenit,' he said defiantly. 'It's a Soviet brand.' Expecting his father to splutter in outrage at his possession of a Communist camera.

But Tony just said, 'They make great lenses, the Eastern Europeans,' and strode on along the hard strip of beach at the surf's edge. Ant floundered through the soft sand a few metres to his father's left. He was damned if he'd move across and walk in his father's footsteps.

Reaching the further promontory Tony stopped, and Ant took a couple of photos. They were too low down however for the view he wanted, looking back over the dunes to include the river estuary. Tony saw his problem, produced the solution. 'If you were to climb that hill ... '

So they clambered up the dunes, and up the nearest hill, but now the sun was in the wrong position, Tony noticed. He thrust on ahead to the next hill, so Ant could get his shot.

Pushing his way through the maze of scrub behind Tony, Ant again found himself hampered by his spectacles, for the ricochet of the branches swinging back behind his father kept nearly knocking them from Ant's face.

At last they reached the second hill and Tony pointed out a place where Ant could tuck himself into the slope to avoid the sun getting into the lens. Ant took the lens cap off, checked the light, focused, clicked, but got no joy from taking the photograph that his father had set up. It wasn't his picture any more.

'Ready to go back to the car now?' Tony inquired politely before spurting ahead again. This time, to avoid the backlash of branches, Ant stayed some distance behind.

And predictably was soon lost.

This scrub was really horrible: sappy green coastal bushes just a little higher than Ant's head, so he couldn't see his way through the maze.

But think now.

Stay calm.

The ocean had to be on that side — didn't it?

And the river had to be over there — hadn't it?

And the car must be ...

It took an hour of burrowing headlong through

tunnels of scrub, following pathways that petered out in gullies, fiddling back and forth, even gazing helplessly up to try to get his bearings from the noonday sun. (If he were a Queen's Scout, he'd have a compass.)

At last out he popped into a clearing that contained the red car and his father.

Tony was peeling a mandarin. He just nodded, tossed another one to Ant.

Ant peeled it. He hated mandarins. Didn't his father remember anything? He'd always hated mandarins, ever since he was a baby. Mum knew that, and never bought them.

(iv) Port Fairy Where the Past is Ever Present

'Port Fairy where the past is ever present,' Ant announced in a stilted reading-around-the-class voice. Tony had asked him to check through the tourist brochures they'd picked up in Apollo Bay, to see what there was to see, where there was to stay. The afternoon was getting on, and they still had twenty or so kilometres to go before they reached Port Fairy. That's where Tony said they would stay for the night.

'Go on,' he urged now.

Ant cleared his throat, but read the article silently.

Port Fairy Where the Past is Ever Present

The Port Fairy district of Victoria is a meeting point for Past and Present, with a unique history going back to the beginning of Time.

Amongst the area's attractions is a rich Aboriginal heritage, as prior to settlement many clans lived in the area. Shell middens right along the coastline provide evidence of Aboriginal camps, especially to the west, in the area of the Crags.

The area awoke from its long sleep in the early nineteenth century, when whalers and sealers from Van Diemen's Land built huts along the Moyne River as a place to shelter during the whaling season. Some of these first settlers married the local women, and the Aboriginal tribes were soon replaced by a thriving community.

In the 1820s a bay whaling station was established on the little island at the river mouth, and was purchased in 1835 by John Griffiths, who gave the island his name.

Soon the East Beach was covered with the massive skeletons of the Southern Right Whales. By the mid 1840s the supply of whales was exhausted and the whaling station was closed.

No trace of it remains today on Griffiths Island, home to a large colony of mutton birds which arrive each September from Alaska to lay their eggs, leaving again for the northern hemisphere in April.

Today, Port Fairy's colourful history is part of the nation's heritage, with over fifty buildings classified by the National Trust. A variety of motels, caravan parks and pub-style accommodation and many excellent restaurants ensure that the town will prove irresistible to lovers of olde worlde charm and modern comfort alike.

'What's it say?' Ant's father asked again.

Ant provided a quick translation: 'Well, for thousands and thousands of years, Koorie people lived here really happily. Then all these white English criminals came over from Tasmania. They raped the Aboriginal women and killed the men, and stole the place. Then they slaughtered out all the whales within twenty years ... '

Ant was watching his father as he spoke, waiting for him to protest at Ant's interpretation so that Ant could weigh in with his beliefs about Land Rights, conservation, the environment. It wasn't that Ant liked fights — quite the opposite, in fact — but it was as if he somehow felt that he had to define the difference between himself and his father, and politics would be the quickest way.

Tony however just kept driving steadily westwards, his eyes on the road. At last he said, 'Go on ... '

'So,' Ant concluded lamely, 'so there's lots of lovely old buildings and heaps of places to eat and sleep.'

'Okay, read through the ads for caravan parks and find us a good one.'

Ant chose one that sounded all right, but when they looked at the on-site van they'd just booked into, it was so filthy that even the curtains were mouldy. They booked out, drove back towards the centre of town, and Tony pulled in at the first motel with a Vacancy sign. He winced as the receptionist told him the price, but pulled out his bankcard. Ant felt bad again about the tent. They'd tried to buy another fly sheet and pole that morning, but there wasn't a disposal shop at Apollo Bay.

There was an hour of daylight left, and Tony thought a brisk walk along the river bank to Griffiths Island would help build up their appetites for dinner.

Ant already felt starving, but said nothing.

The walk was brisk enough, through a high wind that was blowing straight from the South, but when they reached the little causeway to the island it wasn't just the weather that made Ant pull the neck of his jumper up over his nose.

The stench was indescribable.

At first Ant thought it must be the local sewerage outlet, but then he saw the mounds of sea kelp which the recent storms had washed up to rot on the rocks.

There was a sign erected by the Department of Conservation and Environment, warning people to leave pets in the car. Eighty per cent of the mutton bird chicks that hatch on the island die, it said, mostly because of attacks by dogs and cats.

Ant and his father battled out along the track, through wind that seemed intent on pushing them back to shore. On a number of occasions they saw the bones and feathers of a mutton bird that had been savaged to death. Ant thought of the whale carcases, littering the beach.

'The stench of history,' Tony said, turning abruptly back the way they had come. 'The stink of the past.'

It was as if he'd read Ant's mind.

(v) The Evidence

The next morning, at the Crags, history again forced itself upon Ant and his father.

The Crags were outcrops on the coastal rock shelf, framing a little cove of beach. This time, Ant left his camera in the car. Didn't want Tony taking any more photographs through him. And besides, today the thick drizzle had started up again. They did their parkas up tight, pulled hoods over their ears, and headed down the track that followed the small cliff alongside the beach.

Despite the weather, you could see what a great picnic

spot this would be on a good day. And sure enough, vast shell middens beside the track showed how the local people had picnicked here for sixty thousand years or more.

Ant and his father stood silently, looking at the evidence, till the heavens opened and the rain sent the trespassers slithering back to their red car.

(vi) Layers

It was that third night that the storm really started to build up. Ant and Tony were snug inside the pub at Nelson, where the Glenelg River ends its long journey down from Gariwerd and spills into the sea. On the map the straight line of the Victoria/South Australia border ran down through the forest, but the river snaked its way back and forth, heedless of stuff like governments and states.

The travellers ate a counter meal and felt the warmth of the log fire start to dry their muddy jeans.

Afterwards, sitting up at the bar, Ant noticed a boy — well, a man perhaps, but he didn't look much older than Ant. He was short and slight, and was clearly from the city, but Ant observed how all the locals greeted him and asked him, 'Howzitgoin?'

'Okay,' he'd say. 'Bit muddy up top but nice and dry down my hole.'

'You're like an old wombat down a burrow,' the barman told him, and he laughed.

Ant found himself getting more and more curious about why the young man was at Nelson, but it was Tony who shifted his stool a little, made a remark about the weather outside versus the warmth in here, and got around to asking the stranger what brought him to this neck of the woods.

He was a student, he explained, doing post-grad studies in Ecological Archaeology at some Melbourne university, and he was studying a thirty-metre shaft that had been a natural animal trap for twenty thousand years or more.

He was a bit reticent at first, as if he thought Tony's question had just been pub politeness, but Ant's father gently eased out the story. Not only was Tony's whole method quite the opposite from the way television show barristers interrogate someone in court, but it was far easier than the way he talked to Ant.

Ant's mind did one of its out-of-the-body clicks, and he found himself observing the two chatting away at the bar, and thinking how they looked like a father and son who were having a fabulous time on a holiday together. But then who was this other person, who was the spitting image (except for the specs) of the father figure? Why was he sitting by himself, speaking to no one, like the proverbial wet blanket?

'Do you use carbon dating, or is that old hat these days?' Ant heard Tony ask, and he clicked back into the conversation.

It seemed that the young archaeologist was trying to chart climate changes over the last twenty thousand years, as they were revealed by the different animals that had fallen down the hole. His job was carefully to measure the layers of time down his shaft, gently to unearth the skeletons of creatures ranging from tiny lizards to big mammals, then identify them, date them. The ultimate aim, he said, was to be able to project possible climatic patterns of the future. 'Hopefully, anyway,' he concluded.

Tony began to mention some documentary he'd seen, about ancient tree trunks that had been unearthed in a swamp in Tasmania. By slicing through and examining the growth layers, scientists had been able to measure the experience not just of that particular tree but of the whole ecosystem going back thousands and thousands of years ...

If only, Ant thought, it were so easy to slice through the layers of himself and his father; if it were possible to measure in one glance the experience of these last five years, as they had been growing apart. But then, Ant realised, they'd been apart, even when they'd lived together. He had very few memories of living with his father: it was as if those pages of the past were missing.

Later that night, in the pub bathroom, Ant noticed his father touch a fingertip to his eyeball, lift a contact lens, place it in a small white plastic container. On the first two nights, in motels, they hadn't used the bathroom at the same time. Ant felt he was staring, and assiduously brushed at his teeth, but Tony caught his glance in the mirror as he repeated the performance with the second lens.

'It's vanity, I guess,' Tony blushed.

And Ant felt suddenly a little easier with the man, even though his bad eyesight meant there was something else they shared in common.

(vii) A Limestone Gorge and Caves

Over scrambled eggs and bacon, Ant read silently from the brochures put out by the Department of Conservation and Environment.

A Limestone Gorge and Caves

The most spectacular feature of Lower Glenelg National Park is the gorge of the Glenelg River. For 15 kilometres along its lower reaches, the river has cut a gorge, in places more than 50 metres deep, in Miocene limestone.

LAND/SCAPE

Water percolating through and dissolving the limestone has formed caves, which are of archaeological interest. Some caves have vertical shafts which, over thousands of years, have literally been death traps for unwary animals. The remains of long extinct marsupials such as the giant kangaroo and the marsupial lion have been found in these caves, as well as remains of the Tasmanian Devil, now extinct on the mainland.

Ant had believed the student last night but somehow, reading about the archaeology, it seemed more real. It almost made him dizzy to think of time, and the making of the landscape.

'More toast?' Tony asked. 'Or would you like to order a serving of crumpets or muffins or pancakes or something?'

He seemed finally to have realised the size of Ant's appetite; or perhaps he had remembered his own, at that age.

'Yes, please,' Ant said.

'All four?' Tony grinned.

It was only a small joke, but at the beginning of the week it would not have been possible.

Ant smiled back. 'Um, toast,' he said, trying to think of the cheapest. He had never been aware before of how much things cost, but since the other night he'd been watching, and Tony was shelling out about a hundred and fifty bucks a day, what with petrol, accommodation, and Ant's appetite.

Tony pulled a face. 'Oh, go for the pancakes and I'll have some with you. I have toast every morning of my life, living by myself.'

Of the many limestone caves in Lower Glenelg National Park, the main cave of the Princess Margaret Rose Caves is the most attractive. It contains excellent examples of actively growing stalactites, stalagmites, helictites and other spectacular limestone formations. The cave can be readily seen on a caves tour led by an informative National Parks Ranger. Commercial boat tours operate to the caves from Nelson.

'So what's on the agenda for today?' Tony asked as they mopped up pancake with lemon and sugar. 'You choose.'

Outside, the weather was lashing fiercely at the pub's roof. 'How about,' Ant said, 'we catch a boat up the river, and go for a tour of the caves?'

His father didn't look enthusiastic. 'What about a bushwalk instead? The forest is meant to be really great here.'

Ant looked at him as if he were crazy. 'We'd get drenched! And there's probably branches flying all over the place. At least in the boat and the caves we'd be inside.'

Like the first joke, this too was a milestone: Ant had

felt at ease enough to push against his father's will. Perhaps Tony realised this, for he simply shrugged, said, 'Okay, if that's what you really want,' and moved the rest of the pancakes over to Ant's side of the table.

(viii) The Movement of Water

The boat departed (a notice said) at 1.00 pm Victorian time, 12.30 pm South Australian time. Here on the border, life was lived in dual time zones.

As the captain's wife took down the chain to let the queue on board, Ant politely slipped around the dithering groups of grandparents and children, Japanese honeymoon couples, German backpackers and Australian schoolteachers and bagsed one of the two front tables for Tony and himself.

'Good work,' his father said, sliding in beside him.

The boat was a bit like a cafe: a long rectangular room, with ordinary straight walls and a flat ceiling, rows of chairs and laminex-topped tables. At the back of the cabin was a little counter where you could get teabag tea and instant coffee, packets of chips and Minties, but Tony had brought a thermos of brewed coffee from the pub and a fruit cake from the Nelson shop. (The mandarin supply was finished, Ant was pleased to see.) The whole of the front of the cabin was taken up by a huge glass sliding door that looked out on to what would have been the street.

Except in this case it was the river.

The captain's wife cast off from the little deck in front of their window, clasping her coat tight around her, patting at her hairdo as the wind lashed the rain every which way. Then she slid the door open a little and squeezed back into the warmth of the cabin.

There were waves, Ant saw as they headed inland, not just boat wake but waves crisscrossing the river. And the water was — what? — Payne's grey today, and the shadows of the gorge were ...

Ant fumbled in his yellow bag, pulled out his sketch pad and pencils. He just couldn't stop himself.

First a sketch of the landing station, hills and forest in the background. Glenelg River 7/7/93, he wrote.

Then another: of the bridge as they approached it, a cluster of little boatsheds behind. 7/7/93 ...

Then around the bend a little way, a view of the left side of the gorge, a rock jutting out, two trees on top. 7/7/93 ...

Now twisting back with the river's movement, getting looser, a view to the front, the water curving open, a gentle fold of gorge-top. 7/7/93 ...

Snaking again, moving with the flow like a dancer following a rhythm, a quick series of three bends, three inlets, three hills. 7/7/93 ...

Pace building up now, but focus in, a close look at the gorge-side, the tree trunks strong lines with the foliage today taking on the colour of grey river, grey sky, grey rock, 8B pencil. 7/7/93 ...

For some time now Ant had been aware and not aware of people passing from the cabin to the little front deck, pausing to look over his shoulder, observing as he drew; and the presence of his father, not just quiet beside him but almost breathless, as if afraid to break the spell.

Now the grandmother from the seat behind was commenting to Tony, 'Aren't they lovely ... they're so good ... he's so talented, isn't he? Does he have lessons?'

'I don't know,' Tony replied.

'Oh!' said the grandmother, 'Pardon me, I thought you were his father!' and she bristled away.

Then the river did a sudden jive and the view opened leftwards again towards a curving bay, a cluster of brightly painted boatsheds with landing docks and piers. 7/7/93 ...

And again a turn — this time towards the side of the gorge, the striations of the limestone reminding Ant, as he traced them, how the land makes itself in layers, by the movement of water. 7/7/93

And now as Ant again and again wrote the date on

this record of his journey, it too began to assume a significance, as if the seventh day of the seventh month was like the seventh son of the seventh son in the fairytales: possessing a magic of its own.

Time for one more quick sketch (the river itself this time, boat wash, ripples, a submerged branch) as they headed in to the landing for the caves. 7/7/93 ...

(ix) Inside

The people from the boat milled around for a while in the National Parks building, buying tickets and postcards, looking at wall charts that explained the geology:

The Cave

Most limestone caves are formed by water seeping down through cracks and faultlines in the limestone, dissolving the rock and creating fissures and tunnels. The formation of Princess Margaret Rose Caves, however, was assisted by water from the Glenelg River, which worked its way along a faultline for 300 m. This occurred 800,000 years ago when the river was 15 m above its present height. The water scalloped the walls of the cave and wore a reasonably level floor.

How the Formations Form

Rainwater as it seeps from the surface acts as a weak acid to dissolve limestone, producing a solution of calcium bicarbonate.

When this reaches the air of the cave, carbon dioxide is released and calcium carbonate is deposited in the form of calcite crystals. These crystals make up the diverse and spectacular formations of the cave. The different colours are caused by minerals washed down by the rainwater from overlying soil.

As the solution drips from the cave roof, deposited calcium carbonate is left adhering and a stalactite is formed. Solution dripping from a stalactite builds a stalagmite from the cave floor. If a stalactite and a stalagmite join, they form a column, and if that thickens it becomes a pillar.

A bell rang, and a uniformed ranger led the way to a door in the wall.

Ant and his father found themselves at the front of the queue as the ranger ushered the group through the door and down a flight of extremely steep limestone steps. Though this stairwell was floodlit, it was very narrow; with the forty or so other tourists pushing down behind, it did feel as if there was no way back, if you should happen to have second thoughts.

Ant found himself remembering the story of Alice tumbling down the rabbit hole. There was a giddying feeling about this rapid descent.

And then the stairs opened out into a vast cavern, and all that Ant was aware of was a sense of the earth that overcame him.

Though there was Chapel every morning at school, Ant had never felt religious; now he did. But the awe he felt was not at *God* making the earth, but at the *earth* making the earth: it was a sense of bigness and smallness coming together, as Ant became aware of how each and every drop of calcium carbonate was part of this creation process: and it was a sense of a combination of oldness and newness, for if this creation had been happening since the very beginning, it was happening still, all around Ant, at this very second. Stalactites were building unseen ...

All of this produced in Ant such a feeling of wellbeing that he didn't mind the comments of the other tourists around him — 'Look, darling, it's just like Disneyland!' ... 'Oooh, that's a cute one!' ... 'Here's one that looks like a rocket!' — who seemed to regard the cave just as something put there for their amusement. Tony of course wasn't saying any of this stuff; indeed, Ant hadn't heard him say anything since they'd been down here.

'I'll turn the lights out now,' the ranger announced, 'so that you can experience the darkness. Even on a moonless night,' he explained, 'there is always some light in the sky, and your eyes adapt to it. But down here, there is a complete absence of light. Ready?'

'Ooooooooooo!' gasped the crowd as the lights went off.

Pitch — Ant thought, running through the ways he

knew to describe black — pitch black, jet black, inky black, ebony, black as coal, black as a crow, but nothing in his experience was black as a cave.

He revelled in it, and it wasn't just the depth of colour that was extraordinary to him — it was the density, the complete lack of tones. With no light, there was no shadow. Was this what the colour field painters had been aiming at: pure colour?

Again Ant was aware of the tourists around him: the darkness seemed to make them feel a need for comedy, for they were giggling and cracking pathetic jokes.

'*Ooooookie spooooookies ...* ' said the voice of a grown woman.

And then a man cut in abruptly: 'What's that noise?'

'The Monster from the Deep,' the first joker replied.

'No, I'm serious,' the man said.

'Yeah, just listen ... ' said another voice, sounding alarmed.

They all hushed then, and Ant could hear what they meant: there was a terrible sound of breathing, of short loud rasping breaths, as if some huge creature was in the cave with them, ready to pounce.

'*Quick!*' someone yelled. '*Turn on the lights!*'

But it seemed to take a while for the ranger to reach the switch, and during that time the monstrous panting seemed to Ant to get closer and louder.

'*Ahhhhh!*' There was a collective sigh of relief as light flooded the cavern. And then they were all staring around apprehensively.

What was it?

Where was it?

It was Ant who realised. The monster was his father.

(x) Shrinking

Tony stood as if frozen beside a pillar of golden limestone, his face whitish-green and covered (Ant could see) with a film of sweat. The loud breathing was still going on, getting faster and faster. It was clear that Tony was breathing too fast to take in enough oxygen.

'He's hyperventilating,' Ant heard someone say. 'Get him out of here!'

As the ranger gently took Tony's arm, he started to shake his head wildly back and forth. '*I can't I can't,*' he seemed to be saying between huge breaths and — as if against his will — his tall body began to hunch, and now Ant's father became smaller and smaller, shrinking down in front of the stalactite pillar until he was curling at its base like a child.

'Is he always claustrophobic like this?' the ranger asked Ant.

'I don't know,' Ant said, and then found himself

admitting, 'I don't know him very well.'

'C'mon, mate ... ' The ranger bent over the frightened body. 'You really do have to let us help you.'

The ranger and Ant managed to lift Tony to his feet, then slung his arms around their shoulders and struggled their way up the shaft steps and onto the rim of the earth.

(xi) Outside

Tony sat on the bench outside the exit door. He seemed to be concentrating very hard as his breathing changed over from the hysterical panting to something a little slower, a little deeper.

He was still shivering however.

Ant took his parka off, wrapped it around Tony's shoulders, then found himself rubbing up and down Tony's back in long, firm strokes.

Click.

Ant's mind saw this picture, and then imposed over it — or maybe under it — an almost identical picture of a tall thin bloke comforting a sobbing child.

Dad-and-me. That time I got caught in the channel at Nambucca Heads, and he swam in and pulled me out, and he rubbed my back and made me better, and he didn't go crook at me even though he'd told me there was a bad rip today and I was to stay in the camping ground. Click.

So he did take me on a holiday at least once before, Ant realised. He took me camping. He saved my life. What other nice things did he do that I've forgotten?

'Here you go, mate.' The ranger handed Tony a cup of tea. 'Lots of sugar in it. That'll fix you up in no time.'

'Thanks,' Tony said. He looked at Ant. 'Both of you.'

(xii) The Eye of the Beholder

As well as collecting colour words, Ant liked to collect definitions from art books, and would sometimes even scrawl phrases on to the inside flap of his sketch pad. One of these caught his eye as he opened the pad back in the hotel room:

> *Landscape: a view or prospect of rural scenery, such as can be taken in at a glance from a single point of view ... a picture representing such scenery ...*

He had read it a hundred times but now he found himself wondering: what if the same thing was looked at from two completely different viewpoints?

(xiii) Economics

That night in the bar, Ant again saw how easily his father could make friends with people. It was an abalone diver this time, a huge bloke with raw red hands and a scar running from eyebrow to jaw line. Ant watched as Tony got the bloke talking about what he did — where he dived — how big the average catch was — how long he'd been diving — hazards and dangers ...

'Yeah, it can get pretty dicey down there at times,' the diver said.

Tony shuddered. 'I don't know how you can stand it. I'd be hopeless. Got petrified just going down the caves this morning.'

Ant was surprised to hear his father come out with his fear in front of this bloke, but the ab diver nodded.

'Everyone's afraid of something, I reckon,' he said. 'With me it's moths. Put me in a room with a bogong and I'm screaming in five seconds.' He pointed to Tony's glass. 'What're you and the young bloke having?'

'Thanks — a light beer and a Coke.'

Over the next couple of drinks the diver asked Tony what he did for a crust, where he came from, and then the conversation moved back to abalone: prices, the Japanese market, fluctuations in the dollar, the value of the yen.

'Course,' the diver said, 'it's the licence fee that cripples you. The going rate is about a million dollars, before you can put your toe in the water.'

For the first time, Ant spoke. 'A million dollars!'

'They reckon it's to protect the species or something,' the diver said. 'Bloody conservationists.' He made a spitting sound.

Seeing trouble coming, Tony deftly fielded the conversation into a safer direction. 'It's the same in my line of work,' he said. 'It costs an arm and a leg, before you earn a cracker.'

'How come?' the diver asked. 'I'd've thought barristers would be on Easy Street.'

'Oh, some of them,' Tony agreed. 'Some make a packet. But I've always done mostly Legal Aid work, and that's really dried up in the recession. Government just isn't funding it.' He nodded to the publican to order another round. 'But whether I get any work or not,' he went on, 'I've still got to pay three hundred and fifty dollars a week rent for my room in Chambers.'

'Three hundred and fifty bucks a week rent!' the diver exclaimed. 'For one room!'

'Yeah,' Tony grinned. 'And I can't even sleep in it. Still,' he sighed, 'shouldn't complain. There's thousands far worse off.'

'That's for sure, mate,' the diver agreed. 'That's for bloody sure.'

(xiv) The Fine Art of Conversation

Later that night, lying in darkness in their room, Ant listened to the tempest. The roof had come off the fish cannery at Port MacDonnell, the publican had told them, and the harbour was closed at Portland. Some of the old-timers reckoned they couldn't remember a storm quite this bad.

From the other bed, Tony asked tentatively, 'You okay there? Not scared or anything?'

'No,' Ant said. The pub was an old stone building, huddled down into the earth. It felt safe.

But now that Tony had started talking, Ant wanted to keep going, wanted to say something — but how? Even in the dark, it wasn't easy.

Just start ...

'Um,' Ant said.

After a while came the reply: 'Um what?'

'Um, can I ask you something?'

'Go on.'

Losing courage: 'It doesn't matter.'

'Yes it does.'

'No it doesn't.'

Losing patience: 'Come on, Antony. Out with it.'

'Well. Um. You know how you're really broke?'

'No,' said Ant's father. 'I am not really broke. I am just

not really rich.'

'Yeah, well, I was thinking ... '

Silence.

'Thinking what?'

All in a rush: 'Thinking about how, if I changed over to the Creative Arts High School, then you wouldn't have to pay my school fees?'

'I am happy to pay the fees for your school.'

'Yeah but ... '

'I went there, and I am happy for you to go there.'

So that was that. Mum had said not to waste his breath.

Then out it spluttered.

'Yeah but *I'm* not happy to go there. How do you think I feel, going somewhere you went? Hearing about you from the teachers, every day of my life? Looking at your name, on the board in the chapel? Having the same name, and being told all the time that I don't live up to it? How do you think I feel?'

'It was the same for me, remember?' Tony's voice murmured. 'I followed Grandpa there.'

'Yeah, but you were good at the same things as him. I'm different.'

Silence for a moment.

'I just don't fit in there. And anyway, I hate it.'

'Is it that bad?'

'Worse. And I want to go to the Creative Arts School, and learn something useful.'

After a while: 'It was your grandfather that put your name down for the school. Day you were born. I guess I just went along with it.' Silence again. 'I'd have to talk to your mother about it.'

'Thanks, Dad.' It was the first time he'd called his father that for a long time.

Outside, the wind suddenly dropped, as if the storm had blown itself out like a candle.

(xv) Day Five

Pancake time again.

Ant was studying the map. Working out a route that would take them back to Melbourne a different way from how they'd come. His flight went at 4.00 pm. Eight hours from now. Mum would pick him up from Mascot; he'd be home in time for tea. Then he'd have nine days to potter about before school started.

'I guess we could head inland to Winnap,' he read off the map. 'Then up a bit to Casterton. Join the highway and come down through Hamilton, back to Geelong, and up to Melbourne. Or after Hamilton we could just head east towards Ballarat, then come down to Melbourne.'

Tony squeezed lemon over his pancake, sprinkled sugar. 'Which way would you like to go?'

Ant's eyes scanned the map, flicking over exotic place names, blue threads of rivers, green patches of national park, an ochre colour towards the centre ...

'The way I'd like to go,' he joked, 'is straight up north, to the Little Desert National Park, then on from Dimboola, through Hopetoun — there's another national park there — to Ouyen, or however you pronounce it. Up through the Huttah-Kulkyne National Park to Mildura, then all the way up the Silver City Highway to Broken Hill.' Ant laughed, scoffed down his orange juice.

'Okay,' Tony said. 'Better ring your mother and tell her not to meet you.'

'What?' Ant's eyes were on his father. He had to be teasing.

'Why not?' Tony asked. 'You've got another week of holidays, I haven't got any work till August. We can go up to Broken Hill, poke around a bit, and then I can drive you back to Sydney. Check out this school you're so keen on, have a word with Mum about it ... '

'Broken Hill! Do you really mean it?' Ant had read about it in an art magazine: lots of painters lived there. Just from photographs Ant knew why: it was the colours of the landscape. Then he thought of something. 'What about, um, money? Won't a trip like that cost a lot?'

His father smiled. 'We'll cash in your air ticket — that should cover the petrol. And anyway, there should be a disposal store in one of the bigger towns, where we could buy another tent pole and fly sheet. I don't know about you, but I feel like going camping.'

'Great,' Ant agreed, and meant it.

(xvi) Recording the Journey

Heading inland, the road began to open out before the windscreen. Even the sky was getting bigger.

Ant propped his sketch pad against the flap of the glovebox, got out a pencil, began a rapid record of the journey.

Glancing over as the folds of the landscape began to flow across the page, Tony asked, 'How on earth do you do that?'

'It's easy,' Ant told him. 'You just put down what you want to remember.'

THE BLAST FURNACE

On Gramma's bedside table, among the pills and medicines, the metho and tissues and cuttings from the obituary notices, there was a framed motto: 'My Father's house has many mansions.' A few years ago, when Liv had first met Gramma, it used to puzzle her: how could lots of mansions fit inside the one house? It was like saying that a stack of beer cartons could be inside a shoebox. Or that a whole lot of girls could be inside Liv. Now, however, Liv knew exactly how it could happen. For within the single complex that made up the ruins of the old blast furnace, Liv had mansions for all moods and all seasons.

As she approached it now, on this nothing-day when she was in the process of turning fourteen, its solid power reached out to her as it had the very first time she'd seen it.

THE BLAST FURNACE

An autumn afternoon. Liv is ten. Wearing an itchy pink wool dress (pink!) that Mum has specially bought her. ('You can be bridesmaid!' As if that'd reconcile her.) It is too tight. Already at ten Liv is a 14 in women's sizes, but since the Chinese smorgasbord after the registry office the pink dress pulls across her tum.

They drive — well, he drives, Uncle Bruce, that's what Mum says she has to call him — up the highway to the top of the Blue Mountains, then turn off to the right. ('Might as well take the scenic route,' he says. 'I told Ma we wouldn't be back till four.') Now the road goes through gum trees for a while, then zigzags up a steep hill and Liv feels sick. He stops at the top and they get out into a scrubby mess of saplings and charred stubble. The wind bites through the pink dress.

'Thar she blows!' he says.

'Oh darl!' Mum says first to him. 'Oh darl!' she says again to Liv. 'Isn't it going to be exciting, sweetheart, living in the country!'

Liv looks down into a town that huddles in the valley like a trapped beast. Roofs and roofs and roofs, a web of railway lines, mounds of black coal, and above it all a thick dark smear of smoke.

Coming in through the smell of coal fires, Liv feels the red sweet and sour sauce rising to her throat. What'll they be like, her new family? Four boys. ('Four brothers!' Mum had said. 'Won't that be exciting?') Liv hates boys. Boys always tease her, call her Fatso. And a new school. Liv hates school. Kids always tease her, call her Fatso. She hates him too, and hates this town, hates Mum for making her live here ... and then she sees it.

A big brick tower, that rises above the surrounding wasteland. It has arched windows, like princesses lean out of, but it's not all soft and fanciful like fairytale pictures. Nor is it haunted-looking, despite the fact that the roof is missing and the brickwork of the walls is tumbledown and gappy in parts. It is, rather, reassuring — like an elephant, or a cathedral.

When Liv sees it, she suddenly feels as if she has a friend in town.

After that, the rest of this first day is almost bearable.

They park in the street just across from the tower, and four boys (four *brothers*, Mum says) pour out from a weatherboard cottage. ('This is Dougie. Dannie. Johnno. And Bruz.') Inside, in the front bedroom, a skinny old witch inspects her. ('Say hello to Gramma!') Then his mates arrive, with a few slabs of beer and a couple of wives. ('Is that the daughter?' she hears the women whisper over a plate of Saos. 'Big sort of girl, isn't she?' 'She'll wanta be, to stand up to Gordo.')

Gordo? Oh, Uncle Bruce. Bruce Gordon. Mum is Mrs Gordon now, but I told her I wanted to stay Doyle.

'What's your name again, love?'

'Olivia Doyle.'

'O-livia!' Dougie starts, doing the 'O' in an English voice.

'Oh Livia!' Dannie chimes in.

'Oh Livia oh Livia oh Livia!' Johnno and Bruz join the act.

'We call her Liv for short,' Mum apologises.

'*We* call her Fatso for fat,' Dougie mutters and the brothers collapse together in a scrum of laughter.

Liv looks across to the tower of her friend.

As Liv approached now, through the wasteland, past the new sign threatening 'AUCTION. INDUSTRIAL LOTS' and the not-so-new sign promising 'BICENTENNIAL REDEVELOPMENT PROJECT' she was deciding: where today? For on this nothing-day, the season was unclear: not summer, not winter, not really even spring. It kept changing, as she herself had, back home a few minutes ago. Black tracksuit and her khaki army greatcoat; khaki army shorts and her black size XXL t-shirt; or her mid-season outfit of splodged jungle greens with matching top and bottom? She'd decided on the last little number eventually: felt in need of camouflage today. Which hadn't of course helped her escape unnoticed.

'Where you off to, girl?' old gimlet-eyes had screeched through the flyscreen that divided her bedroom from the front sleep-out, where Liv dwelt.

'Over the blast furnace, Gramma.'

'Have you done your chores?'

'Yeah, Gramma.'

'Your mother know?'

'Yeah, Gramma.'

'You'll fall down one of them holes over there one of these days, girl, and that'll be the finish of you.'

'Yeah, Gramma.'

It was true — the site was riddled with holes. Huge gaping ones and thin slitty ones, and in one place the land fell down a kind of cliff into a large stagnant pond. There were tunnels too, that might fall in, and lots of broken bricks to lose your footing on, and twisted pieces of rusty tin to give you tetanus. The boys were forbidden to go there — last time they had, Gordo had taken off his belt — so it was the one place where Liv could get away from them. And apart from the odd tourist who'd drive in, take one look, and drive off again, no one else ever went there either. It was Liv's place.

So, where today? Her mood, like the weather, was uncertain. Not quite in need of the Cry Cave, where she could huddle inside the earth, but not cheerful enough for Hilltop Grove, where fruit trees grew wild and the breeze blew fresh on your face. And not the Summer House, and not the Winter Quarters. Not the Dwarf Tunnels and not the Dragon Lair. Not the Chicken Coop and not the Elvey Dell and not, definitely not, Snake Lake.

In the end, it was the Tower that she chose, for she was feeling somewhat princessy despite the need of a fairy godmother this morning.

This morning. Wake at dawn as usual, even though it's Saturday, for the witch wakes then, and rattles at the flyscreen for her cuppa.

No need to dress, Liv goes to bed in her tracksuit, for the front sleep-out isn't insulated and the nights are freezing still.

Creep along the hall to the kitchen, throw some kindling onto the smoulders of last night's coal in the stove, boil the kettle (there is an electric one, but the stove takes longer), make the tea — not-too-strong-not-too-weak, girl, beats me how you can get it wrong every time — spread marge on two slices of bread, cut the crusts off (she doesn't put her teeth in till after her metho rub-down at half past eleven).

For a thrill today (Happy Birthday!) Liv puts a flower on the tray.

'What's that then?'

'A daisy, Gramma.'

'Take it away. You know I can't abide flowers in a sick room.'

She sips the tea. 'Beats me how you can get it wrong every time, girl.'

Good. I'm glad you said that. Glad you say it every morning, because every morning I need reminding how much I hate you if I am to hold my breath and do the next thing; because to do the next thing I need an emotion more powerful than disgust.

And so now Liv takes a deep breath then clamps her mouth shut and blocks the air-lock to her nose, then lifts up the seat of the commode, reaches in for the green enamel potty, and carries it (can't go too fast or you'll spill it) all the way down the hall (lungs yelling for air like a diver's) and out to the dunny, and at last tips it down.

At least today she hasn't done number twos. (Happy Birthday Liv!)

But the sound of the flushing wakes Bruz, who wakes Johnno, who wakes Dannie, who wakes Dougie, and Liv storms into the back sleep-out and tries to bribe them with toast, for Mum really needs some sleep (Liv heard her up in the night nursing Gramma) and Liv is damned if the little buggers (sorry, brothers) will wake

Mum before seven at least.

But the toaster only takes two slices at a time and there are four boys and Liv only has two hands, and it's not long before Mum comes out, her faded chenille dressing gown clutched around her. 'Need a hand, darl?'

'No, Mum, you have a bit of a lie-in, I'll make you a cuppa in a minute ...'

But Mum stays anyway, pours the dregs from the teapot.

'For Christ's sake Mum, make a fresh pot.' I wouldn't wish the witch's tea on a dead dog.

But if Liv is a saint, Mum is a martyr, and so she drinks the lukewarm leafy brew, and drinks it black, because Dougie has got to the fridge behind Liv's back and finished off the milk.

'I'll go up the shop and get some,' Liv says.

When she gets back, Mum is dressed, and remembers. 'Oh Liv. I forgot. It's not much I'm afraid, but darl, you know how it is.'

Yes, I know. There's a recession on. The Treasurer said it the other night on TV. So now there's an official reason for the way this whole town hurts, and Liv's family with it.

Liv opens the package that has been carefully wrapped in recycled Santa Clauses. Two hair doodahs — one shocking pink and the other a kind of purple and cerise and yellow. A pair of tights. A copy of the latest Sweet Dreams. And an IOU for '1 pair Good Shoes'.

'It's from all of us,' Mum lies.

'Oh Mum. Ta.' Mum has tried, and Liv knows it, but the present is for a girl who ties back her long fine hair with doodahs, for a girl who clads her long thin legs in tights, for a girl who dreams of romance as she totters on Good Shoes to the ball; for a girl who is not Liv. 'But if you don't mind I'll use the IOU for a pair of runners.'

Mum is disappointed. Liv wears thongs in summer, an old pair of work boots in winter, and Mum has been nagging about Liv's footwear for ages. But 'Oh well, it's your funeral,' Mum sighs. 'Happy birthday, darl.'

'Ta, Mum.'

After a proper breakfast (eggs sausages bacon and tomato) has been cooked for Gordo, and the first load of washing has been hung out, Mum and Liv do the weekly supermarket shopping, carry it all the way home. (Gordo takes the boys to footie on Saturday mornings, not that Mum can drive anyway. But he could at least pick us up, Liv thinks as the plastic carry-bags cut through her hands.)

Liv unpacks while Mum goes in to give Gramma her rub-down, then it's time to change the sheets on the boys' bunks (they're fixed to the wall so it's hard to tuck in the top ones; and when you do the bottom ones you always forget, and crack your head). While the sheets are in the machine, run the vac round the back sleep-out, avoiding the race track, sucking up Lego. Now hang the sheets out.

'Heavens!' Mum emerges exhausted and smelling of metho. 'Is that the time?'

Put the pies in the oven, the boys'll be home from footy in a moment, skiting and starving.

'Anyway, I scored a try!'

'I scored two tries!'

'Where's lunch?'

'Anyway, I kicked a goal!'

'I'm hungry!'

'When'll lunch be ready?!'

'Honestly,' Gordo complains to Mum, 'I can't see why you can't have the pies hot for when the boys get home.'

'It's my fault,' Liv says. 'I forgot.'

'You forget every bloody week,' Gordo says. 'Anyone'd think it was deliberate.'

'They'll be ready any minute now,' Mum promises.

So the boys disappear on their bikes, and Liv rinses the worst of the mud off their footy gear and puts it in the machine, and when the boys finally get back the pies are a bit burnt on top and there's another scene. Liv takes the best two out to Gordo, who is washing the car. Puts the plate on the bonnet.

'Mind the bloody duco! What, have these been through a bushfire or something!'

Liv takes the worst two pies round the back of the laundry. The hills that surround the town press in on her, trapping her, while the coal smoke hangs above like a lid. It is not that today is worse than any other Saturday, but that it is exactly the same. This has been going on for ever, and it will go on for ever and ever and ever amen.

The machine gives a thump to say that it is time to hang out the footy gear, bring in the first load of dry stuff.

'Never mind, darl,' Mum tells Liv's long face. 'It might never happen.'

It has it has it already has. And it will it will it will.

Liv gets out the ironing board.

'I'll do that, darl.'

Mum looks dead weary after this morning's session with Gramma. 'It's okay. You go and have a lie-down, read the paper.'

Liv actually smiles as she starts on Gordo's work shirts. Only half an hour and *World of Sport* will be on, and they'll all sit there mesmerised, and Cinderella will escape.

Arriving at the Tower, Liv bypassed the steps that led

THE BLAST FURNACE

up to the broad archway of the front entrance and clambered up a mound of rubble to one of the two narrower arches at the eastern side. Her head spun for a moment, for the floorboards of the old power house were completely missing and it was a long drop to the bottom of the machine pit. Down below was a mess of broken bricks, rusty pieces of tin, corroded piping, an old fridge, even a holly tree.

'You'll fall down one of them holes and that'll be the finish of you!' the witch's curse rang in Liv's head.

That's what you think!

Facing inwards to the arch and clinging for balance, Liv stretched her right foot across the gap to the top of a brick pier, about two metres square, that had once provided the base for one of the engines. Took a deep breath, leant all her weight onto this first foot, brought the left foot over to join it.

Secure now on her platform, Liv danced to the music of her Walkman ('This is Radio 2LT Lithgow,' said the man. 'Rock till you drop!') and as her energy filled the space, the Tower itself seemed to remember the enormous power of its past.

There's a black and white photograph on Liv's sleep-out wall, that she cut out of the paper on Heritage Day '88. It shows the tower as it once was, standing proudly with its roof on and its bricks all clean and fresh. To its left, there is a little building that looks like a church hall. To its right, the massive cylinder of the furnace itself looms above the heating stoves. Beyond this again, the great pillar of the steam hoist rises up in front of a chimney so tall that it disappears out of the top of the picture. Running between all these structures is a network of gigantic pipes. And crowded in front of all this there are the ant specks of hundreds of people.

Underneath, the caption says:

> On 13th May 1907, Australia's first blast furnace was blown in and tapped in the presence of the Premier and a train-load of dignatories. Fortunately, the noise of the furnace was too great to allow for speechmaking.

And now it is that day, and Liv pulls the switch inside the power house, and there is a piercing whistle and a belch of smoke and Liv feels the earth shudder as air pushes through the pipes and the metal flows red and molten and the great creature comes to life ...

When Liv woke, lying on the platform where she'd danced herself into exhaustion, there was an old woman sitting in the archway of the front entrance with a bunch of scarlet poppies in her lap. For a moment, Liv thought it was the witch come to worry her, and then she thought she was asleep still and dreaming the witch, and then she realised that it was just an old woman wearing a yellow baseball cap and a blue tracksuit and eating a green Granny Smith apple.

The woman's lips moved, but Liv had gone deaf. The lips moved again and the woman threw an apple at her. Then Liv realised that she'd turned the radio off but left the ear plugs in. She pulled them out now and heard 'Don't you?'

'Yes,' Liv said, wondering what she had agreed to, and bit into the apple to be polite.

The woman was skinny, but triangular as she sat cross-legged on the top step, and really very old, Liv saw, and her hair was long and there were yellow streaks in the white and her lipstick was as red as the poppies that she indicated now.

'Thought you must've been into these,' she said.

Huh?

'When you slept so sound.'

Huh again? Liv had seen the poppies growing around the edge of the ruins but they were just —

'Opium poppies,' the old woman said. 'Mind you, I only pick 'em for the colour, I *like* flowers, but there's others who might use 'em for, you know.'

'Not me,' Liv said quickly,

'There's a good girl,' the woman agreed. 'What you say

your name was again?'

'Olivia Doyle.'

The woman's forehead creased. 'Doyle. Doyle. Wouldn't be Charlie Doyle's girl, would you?'

'No. Sorry.' Doyle was Mum's name. Liv didn't know her dad's name. That was all long gone and best forgotten, Mum always said in the days when Liv used to ask. 'I don't come from round here.'

'Tourist job eh?'

'No, I mean ... I live across the block there. At Gordon's. Bruce Gordon. He's my' (choke on the word) 'stepdad.'

The woman creased up her face again. It was as if it were vital for her to place Liv. '*Bruce* Gordon? Bruce *Gordon*?' The light seemed to dawn. 'That wouldn't be Menie Gordon's boy, by any chance?'

Liv tried to think. She was just Gramma. Or Old Mrs Gordon. On her tablet bottles the initial was W. 'Menie?' Liv asked.

'Short for Wilhemina. We called her that because she was such a bitch. Oh! Pardon my French!'

'That's her,' Liv said.

'Well fancy! Menie Gordon still alive and kicking! Course, I am myself, but then I haven't stopped in the one place long enough for Death to catch me.'

Liv was a bit embarrassed by someone saying Death like that. 'Don't you live here now?'

'Me? Here?' The stranger snorted. 'Oh no, the *world's* my oyster, love. Here today, gone tomorrow, that's my motto. Why, only ten days ago I was up at Kakadu — that was for my annual holidays, mind. Coupla weeks before that, I was in Kununurra for the mangoes. Month before that, it was Nambour for the strawberries ...'

Liv was mystified.

'I'm a picker, see, love?' the woman explained. She reached in her pocket and lobbed a tiny green booklet over the gap to the platform. 'Here, this is my Bible.'

Oh no, thought Liv, she's going to ask me to love Jesus.

But the booklet was called *Harvest Table Australia, Summary of Seasonal Crops Requiring Labour.* Inside, there was a calendar for every state, with lists showing all the crops and where they grew. Liv didn't usually like books but this one was poetry to her. As she scanned the lists she could smell the fruit, feel the morning dew, even hear the laughter and friendship of the other pickers as they worked their way along the rows:

Peaches	Pears	Apples	Oranges
Apricots	Tomatoes	Zucchinis	Cherries
Ginger	Grapes	Onions	Capsicums
Lettuces	Potatoes	Bananas	Berries

And when the abundance became too overwhelming she could see the country towns with their wide main streets and lacy pub verandahs, as the rhythm of the place names built a pattern of its own:

> Griffith, Orange, Leeton, Batlow,
> Stanthorpe, Berri, Robin*vale*,
> Coorow, Collie, Moora, Wagin,
> Grass Patch, Dalmore, Innis*fail*!

> Moora, Northam, Wee Waa, Williams,
> Red Hill, Silvan, Manji*mup*,
> Scottsdale, Ingham, Invergordon,
> Healesville, Cobram, Baling*up*!

'Just goes to show,' the old woman was saying, 'you can pick anywhere you go in this land of plenty! You can keep that book if you like, love. Course,' she added, 'that's just the big crops, like, the basics. On top of that you have all the specialist stuff — avocadoes and asparagus, tamarilloes, kiwi fruit and figs, even herbs now that cooking's gone posh. And since this bush tucker craze, they're setting up plantations of lilli pilli and what have you. And then of course' (she winked) 'there's always the illegal ...'

Liv stared across the top of the holly tree.

'Oh yes, I've been asked to pick that marijuana more

than once in my life, love. Did it too, on one occasion, when the engine of the old bongo van blew up and I was stuck with no money in the backside of the universe. Course, those Mafia-types like little old ladies. They know we won't nick the heads. Oh, I'm not proud of myself for doing it but I don't lay awake at nights over it either, mind. I mean, if you're going to think like that, how many alcoholics have I helped by picking grapes? Eh? It's people's *own* decision what they do with their lives, I maintain.'

As for now: 'I'm waiting on the cherries down in Young. They'll start in a day or so. And seeing as I was in the area, I thought I'd drop in on my old haunts.'

Liv was reeling. Could only start with what was nearest at hand. 'How do you think *they* got here? The poppies?'

'Oh?' The woman seemed to have forgotten them. 'Brought by birds maybe. Amazing how birds will spread a plant. Perhaps some bird lived up in that Golden Triangle or whatever they call it, Thailand, somewhere like that, and this bird ate a seed, and carried it down here in her belly, then done a poop and Bob's your uncle.'

Liv reeled even more. To imagine a piece of Thailand (she remembered a TV documentary: water buffaloes and golden Buddhas; rice fields and refugees) here in

Lithgow!

'More likely,' the old woman said, 'some hippy came here, playing Johnny Poppyseed.'

Don't, Liv thought, don't squash my illusions.

For a moment there, the hills that surround the town had receded, and Liv's landscape had opened up to include Mareeba and Marradong, Kyabram, Kakadu, the Golden Triangle, the World.

'Course, she *had* to get married,' the old woman said.

(Who, what, huh?)

'She was C of E of course, while all us were Presos or Methos or even worse, tykes. Menie Wilson that was. Oh and all la-de-da, you wouldn't credit it! As a kid she'd be dressed in white broderie anglaise of a Sunday, with pale blue ribbon pulled through the eyelets in the cloth. Oh and love! Her mother used to copy the patterns for her dresses from what the princesses in England were wearing. She'd copy them from the magazines, and Wilhemina Wilson used to tell us that she was a princess! And the cream of it was, she thought it was true!'

Liv blushed for her own fantasy: but at least it had just been a game for her. (Hadn't it?)

'And her dad working across here at the blast furnace like my dad, and everybody's dad,' the woman went on. 'Least, while they had work. Ha! And meanwhile, for all the posh clothes, she mostly never took any lunch to school. Now, we didn't mind sharing, it was share and share alike here in Lithgow. But the Wilsons, they used to share when you had it, and not share when they did, see? That's why we called her Menie. We'd share our lunch and she wouldn't.

'And then, when we girls grew up a bit, we'd share our dresses for the dances, and we'd share our beaus too. We didn't like to leave a girl standing as a wallflower, just cause she was fat and plain, like Menie Wilson was. So we'd tell our partners: go and dance with her.

'And they would. And she'd steal them. Out the back of the hall and never come back.

'Now there was some who said Menie Wilson was no better than she should be, though I for one never believed them, I mean, Princess Wilhemina in her broderie anglaise and all! But then one day it was announced: next Saturday at St Pauls, the marriage of Wilhemina Wilson, daughter of blah blah, and Douglas Gordon, son of et cetera.

'The Gordons, see, were a Preso family hereabouts, and very God-fearing, and it was said that Menie Wilson only got Dougie Gordon to go to the altar with her because old Mr Gordon was an Elder of the Church. I mean, there were lots of others in the queue, but it was Dougie Gordon copped it. Course, that's all ancient history now.'

Not quite, Liv thought, remembering how the witch had come oh-la-de-da over Mum on many an occasion, and over Liv for only having Mum's name.

'But you said about the blast furnace. Your dads working here.' Liv was still trying to imagine it all blasting and furnacing away. 'What was it like?'

'Like?'

Earth shudders. An engine throbs upon its pier. Coke burns inside the stoves. Air blasts through pipes and tunnels. Smoke belches out the flues. Molten iron, red hot, pours down through the furnace and out into the slits and channels and pools. And above it all, the noise roars through your Summer House and your Winter Quarters, through Hilltop Grove and Elvey Dell. This isn't a playhouse, girl. Think of the photograph.

'Like? It just *was*. And then suddenly it wasn't.'

'Suddenly? Wasn't?' Liv had never really thought about its end, but had somehow imagined it slowly, slowly, subsiding back into the earth ...

'Don't you know, love? Late 1920s it was, start of the Great Depression, they just closed down the industry here, and everything moved to Port Kembla, down near Wollongong. By Christmas 1929, I remember, this whole site here was a ruin ...'

Liv reeled. To think that the power of something as great as the blast furnace could be broken, snap, like a twig.

'And speaking of moving,' the stranger was saying, getting up from the step, 'I'd better be making camp for the night ...'

Alone now, in near darkness, the ruins that surrounded Liv felt for the first time like — ruins. And she felt helpless and betrayed. If the blast furnace could be beaten so easily, what hope had she: a fat, plain, ordinary girl?

Walking back across the wasteland, Liv noticed that there was a tarpaulin strung out from the roof of the yellow bongo van, and that the old woman was setting up a camping stove on a card table, on which the poppies sat in a jam jar.

She's senile, Liv told herself. She's a crackpot, a weirdo, a nutter, a real loony.

Back home, the click of the flyscreen door unleashes the tirade.

'Where've you been girl? Waltzing back in, free as you please, at this hour! Look at her will you ...' Gramma was in her wheelchair in the lounge room with the others, and making the most of her audience.

'... Butter wouldn't melt in her mouth. But you can't tell me she's been off by herself all afternoon ...'

(Ha! If only you knew!)

'... Oh no, like mother like daughter ...'

Mum flinches, but Liv is impervious now to Gramma's slanders. For if Liv is not a princess, and the tower is not a tower, then the witch is not a witch, and cannot harm her.

'... No better than she should be ...'

(If only you knew what I know about you!)

Liv goes to the kitchen and makes herself a bowl of cornflakes, takes it to the sleep-out and eats it in bed.

Waking from a dream she can't quite remember (a beach, was it? Something wide and open, full of sky?), it seems only minutes later but must be hours, for the house is quiet and a shaft of moonlight funnels in through the louvres.

Idly, just wondering, Liv rummages through her school bag and pulls out the geography text. There's a map of Australia printed across the front endpaper. She finds SYDNEY, then Lithgow, in tiny letters, a bit to the left. No Port Kembla ... but here's Wollongong, just below Sydney on the coast. She measures the distance between Lithgow and Wollongong: about 250 kilometres, checking against the map's scale.

And now the fact that earlier had made Liv so

desolate reverses its meaning, and she thinks: if a bloody great blast furnace can get out of the valley and start a new life somewhere ('*It's people's own decision,*' something says in Liv's head *'what they do with their lives*') then so can I, Fat Liv.

Oh not tonight — or rather today, because it is after midnight and the wretched un-birthday is over — but one day. In a year, or maybe two. Liv will put on her runners and go! And in the meantime she will plan her journey.

Gazing still at the map, Liv gets out the Harvest Table and traces her way through the litany of names till the continent alone is too small for her, and she is forced to flip to the back endpaper, where the whole world awaits her like an oyster (Liv giggles) lying open on its shell.

Through the flyscreen, Liv hears Gramma start to call for Mum, and goes in. 'Upsadaisy!' she bosses as she lifts the bag of bones onto the commode.

Stepping out onto the verandah while she waits for Gramma, Liv sees a spurt of flame, gold-blue, across at the ruins, and thinks she is imagining it until she remembers the gas stove. The thought makes Liv sniff, but it is not gas that she can smell, or the usual coal smoke of Lithgow, for the breeze that blows across from the blast furnace seems to carry a faint tang of salt.

THE PRODIGAL

It is Mum on the phone that sets this off:

'Marta, it's Mum ...'

Before I can get to 'Hi Mum, how are you?' she starts the conversation again:

'Marta, it's about Maree ...'

Maree.

Of course it's about Maree.

It is always about Maree.

And always has been.

In the beginning there was Maree. And for ever and ever Amen there will be Maree too.

As Mum talks away in my ear I doodle a design for the window of the east chapel, and imagine how the conversation might have gone ...

'Marta, it's Mum ...'

'Hi Mum, how are you?'

'Fine, love, and yourself?'

'Great, Mum, just great.' Then, bursting with excitement: 'Mum, I got the St Paul's job! My first window!'

'Your first window by yourself! And at St Paul's! Oh Marta!' She gushes on for a while, says of course I've always been *so* artistic, asks what sort of thing they want ...

'Something modern. But pictorial. You know — storytelling. And cheerful, they reckon.'

'Cheerful? I guess that means New Testament.'

'The Crucifixion was hardly cheerful.'

'Oh well, you can always leave that bit out,' she suggests.

'It is rather the point of the book.' (Why, even in my imaginary conversations with my mother, do we always end up arguing?)

But Mum (as always) talks over me. 'What about the Parables? Or the Miracles? Now *they're* nice ...'

'Oh yeah. Delightful. I could do everyone getting pissed at the marriage at Cana.'

'Marta!'

'Or perhaps the Prodigal, wasting his substance with riotous living. You know — unsafe sex, dirty needles, the full bit.'

'Marta, really!'

As my fantasy conversation gets wilder and wilder,

the real mum continues the real talking into my ear, and I realise that my doodle really is a picture of the Prodigal. Which isn't surprising I suppose because, looking back, it was the Prodigal that got me into all this ...

It wasn't till Maree left that the family started going to church.

No, to say it like that is wrong, for once Maree left there was no family, just three peas rattling in a two-bedroom brick veneer pod: Mum, frantic in a monotonous way, obsessive, driven; Dad, even more withdrawn than usual, damp-eyed, wooden; and me, genuinely worried of course (Had she been murdered? Or even raped?) but also secretly enjoying having the bedroom to myself, and resentful that now Maree was gone, she seemed to get even more attention than she had when she was there. (Dad and Mum would spend every Friday and Saturday night driving slowly around the city, staring at kids on street corners, sticking photograph posters on lamp posts: HAVE YOU SEEN THIS GIRL? Meanwhile I'd be at home, eating things in tins for tea, forbidden to go out *in case the phone rings*.)

She left in February, just after term started (she was in Year 11, I was in Year 9) and we were regular parishioners of the local Uniting Church by Easter.

THE PRODIGAL

(Uniting. I hated even the name of our religion. It was so humdrum and wishy-washy. If we had to crawl to God to get Maree back, I thought, why couldn't we at least do it more colourfully? I'd been once to Greek church with my friend Effie: priests with long beards and pillbox hats and lots of candles and lovely incense. And I'd seen American sorts of churches on TV, with rock-and-roll singing and people throwing themselves on the floor and yelling out really interesting sins. But even when following the Lord, my parents took the middle road.)

That Easter, I remember, was when the minister began including Maree in the special prayers of the congregation. Along with the Queen and the missionaries and the people in hospital we would get:

> Almighty and everlasting God
> who alone works miracles,
> please grant us the safe
> return of Maree, beloved daughter
> of Ron and Elaine Powell, and
> sister of Marta.

I would blush bright red and hope none of the guys from Fellowship was looking at me.

The only thing that made church bearable was the windows. I would spend the time gazing up, watching the light stream down through the coloured glass. At that time it was the tones, the shift and change of red and gold and blue that absorbed me. I knew nothing of art, didn't even think to wonder whether the figures were clumsy or skilful, whether the compositions worked or not. I didn't, in the beginning, even think of the pictures as having meaning. How could I? I didn't know the stories when we started going to church. It was only after a few months of Bible readings and sermons that I was able to work out what was going on.

There, in the round window at the centre, was Jesus with his arms out, bordered by the wording of one of the Beatitudes: 'BLESSED ARE THE MEEK' (above) 'FOR THEY SHALL INHERIT THE EARTH' (below).

Ha ha de ha ha! I used to think. Being one of the meek myself, I knew that was bullshit.

Flanking this there was a sort of Before and After shot of the Prodigal Son. On the left, he'd gone to the far country and spent his inheritance and now he was dressed in rags, feeding swine, looking hungrily at a corn cob that one of the pigs was gobbling. On the right he was back home again, clothed in the best robe, and you could see his father behind him calling out, 'Bring hither the fatted calf and kill it, and let us eat and be merry: for this my son was dead, and is alive again; he was lost, and is found.'

I of course always identified with the Prodigal's brother, who came home from the field and saw the party going on and complained to the father that *he* had always stayed home and been good, and yet *he* had never been given a barbecue so he could be merry with his mates.

But despite my rejection of the theology of the picture, I was hooked on the idea of telling a tale through coloured glass.

I guess it was about September, October — Maree had been gone seven or eight months or so — that I saw the ad in the local paper (underneath MISSING. MAREE POWELL. PLEASE COME BACK. WE LOVE YOU. MUM, DAD & MARTA.) for evening classes in leadlight at the local scout hall.

Leadlight.

The very word somehow made my head spin. The combination of lead, that was heavy, and light, that was — well, light.

'Could I go?' I begged. The classes were on Friday nights, so they wouldn't interfere with my homework. And the scouts hall was just on the corner, so I could walk home safely and wouldn't be — I couldn't say what I wouldn't be, because that might remind them of what Maree might have been. Kidnapped. Raped. Murdered and lying now in thick bushland. Like the body that

Dad had had to go to the morgue and identify, or as it turned out (thank-the-Lord-I-don't-believe-in) *not* identify a couple of months before.

No, Mum said straight out. How could I even ask?

On Friday nights Mum and Dad had to drive slowly around the streets of the city, staring at the faces of the kids who hung about the corners, and I had to stay home in case the phone rang. Didn't I know that? Didn't I care about Maree?

Yes, but ... (I actually didn't believe she'd ring, any more than I really believed she'd been kidnapped. She'd taken her coat, and a sleeping bag, and all her jewellery, and my twenty dollars, when she'd gone. Though of course she might subsequently have been ... But then she certainly wouldn't ring.)

It was Dad who came to the rescue. He said he'd do the driving and looking by himself on Fridays, and Mum could stay home and mind the phone. He said he thought two nights of looking was too hard on Mum anyway, what with her blood pressure.

So I started the classes, and within a week I was as obsessed with leadlight as Mum and Dad were with the searching. I guess, looking back, it was my way of escaping the pain.

At the back of the house there was a little verandah, and I set up an old table there and my soldering stuff and I would spend hours, days, drawing the cartoons, cutting the glass, sticking the lead around the edges, then jigsawing the pieces together. At first I was copying designs from a book, and it was satisfying just to get all the pieces to fit when everything else in the world seemed out of kilter. Soon however I was doing my own designs — rough, clumsy, but done by me, Marta Powell. I say I was obsessed with it, but a better term might be addicted. And, like any addict, I needed money for my fix. In order to buy the glass to make the pictures, I had to sell the pictures I made. So I started up a Saturday stall at one of the inner city markets. Mum actually approved: lots of street kids went to the markets, and she made me promise to have one of the Maree posters on the stall. Embarrassing, but I did it.

In return, Dad would drop me and my gear at the market before he started his Saturday daytime search, then pick me up and drop me home (to mind the phone!) before he and Mum set off for the night shift.

Meanwhile, the next Easter came and went, and I was in Year 10. I'd always been one of the dodos at school before this: just passing, or just failing, not popular, but not hated, just some sort of quiet blob that no one particularly noticed. That had changed of course when Maree went missing. For a month or so, when it first happened, I was notorious. Teachers, even Year 12 kids, would stop me in the playground and ask: '*Any news?*' I felt like getting a cassette recorder and taping the answer: '*No ...*' '*Not yet ...*' '*Not really ...*' Eventually, the questioning died down, but a bit of ghoulish fame clung to me. After all, *I* was the girl who was the sister of the girl whose body might be ...

The pain of it all of course was that I was still in her shadow. But without her presence I did maybe seem a little more something in myself. Before, it had been as if she were the positive, and I were the negative. She was sharp, vivid, with a cloud of fizzy gold spiral curls and a face that was all movement. I was stodgy, stolid, with limp brown hair that just sort of flopped down in strands over the broad bones of my cheeks. Now that she was gone, my looks didn't of course do a Before-and-After, but somehow I felt less dull.

Or maybe it was the glass that made the difference. Now that I was working with colour, through colour, perhaps something of the light alchemised into my soul. All I know is that I started doing better at schoolwork (before it had been Maree of course who was brilliant, though slack as slack).

The crunch came just after the Year 10 exams, when it was my turn to see the careers adviser.

'You've done quite well, Marta ...' I could hear the surprise in her voice. 'Have you any idea what you'd like to do — whether you want to stay on at school ...'

In those days, before the recession got so bad, it was normal for heaps of kids to leave at the end of Year 10. Only the bright ones (the ones like Maree) went on to Year 11 and 12. I'd always imagined myself leaving, maybe being a waitress or a shop assistant. But now I found myself saying 'Yes. I do know what I want to do. I want to make church windows.'

Mrs Whalan stared. 'But no one does that, Marta. I mean, maybe in the past, when the old churches were being built ...'

'Well, maybe the windows in the old churches break sometimes, and have to be mended. Or maybe new churches sometimes need leadlight windows.'

Mrs Whalan looked very doubtful. She didn't have any pamphlets. But over the next week she got me to bring in some of my work and show it to the art teacher, and then she made inquiries and said the best thing would be to stay on at school and do Year 11 and 12, and then go to Art School and do leadlight as part of a course. It would probably still be impossible ever to get a job making church windows, but perhaps I could teach leadlight to people wanting a hobby.

'Okay,' I said. I would have agreed to anything, just to keep on working with coloured glass.

Mum and Dad didn't seem to care either way when I

told them, but as a special reward for my good Year 10 results they gave up a Friday night of searching to come to the end-of-year prize giving. I didn't win anything of course, but a couple of my pieces were on display in the front hall and it felt like a prize, having Mum and Dad go out at night for me.

There was supper after the speeches and Mrs Whalan and the art teacher talked for a long time to Dad. Mum sat in a corner, unable to eat anything, holding back her tears. She knew a lot of the Year 12 kids of course, because they'd been Maree's friends, and all the way home in the car she kept saying she couldn't help thinking that if things had been different, Maree would have been among them. She'd probably have been dux, or school captain, or at least won the English prize — she was always so good at poetry ...

It was a wet night, and I remember observing the way the yellow street lights along the freeway made a series of golden haloes, like flowers in a field of dark. If I could capture *that*, I thought.

By the time we got home it was pouring. We parked in the garage, then made a dash up the path towards the back verandah. Sitting there on my leadlight table, sheltering from the rain, was Maree.

'Where have you guys been?' she said. 'I've been waiting for hours.'

THE PRODIGAL

When the Prodigal Son returned, his father had compassion and ran, and fell on his neck and kissed him. In our story it was the mother, but the rest was the same.

Mum took Maree in, and put her in a hot bath, and clothed her in my quilted dressing gown, then fed her cocoa and raisin toast.

'No questions, okay?' Maree threatened.

I saw Dad crying with happiness as he watched the toast.

'I've said I'm sorry,' (she hadn't, actually) 'but I just don't want any hassles. Okay?'

And of course it was. They were scared that if they said something she'd go again. So they said nothing at all.

That Sunday when the three of us went to church (Maree was still asleep) the congregation gave thanks to Almighty God for answering its prayers.

Now, of course, Maree and I were sharing the bedroom again, but at least I had my leadlight work table on the verandah and I could escape out there, and didn't have to watch her lolling on the bed through the long summer days, examining her fingernails, leafing through a *Dolly* magazine, laying out a game of Patience, braiding her hair into dozens of skinny plaits and unbraiding it again. Maree could always think up a hundred and one ways to do absolutely nothing; still can, in fact. (Dad sometimes used to call her 'Lil', short for Lily, from the bit in the Bible where Jesus says to consider the lilies of the field who never toiled or did the chores.)

It was towards the end of January that Maree did one of her crawly-crawlies to Mum and Dad and said she'd seen how stupid she'd been, and she'd decided to go back to school.

'Go back!' I yelled when they told me. 'To *my* school!' If she went back now, she'd be in Year 11, the same as me. It had been bad enough, having her two years ahead, but if she was in the same year!

'It was Maree's school before it was your school,' Mum pointed out. 'Besides, Maree will be able to help you. She's so good at poetry and things.'

One Saturday just before first term started I took a few pieces to the market as usual. Now that Dad didn't search for Maree I had to go on the train, but I'd made a special portfolio and could (just) carry it. When I got home, late that afternoon, I could hear the noise from the street.

It turned out that Dad had invited the church Men's Club to our place for a working bee. He'd provided the materials, and they'd been flat out all day extending the back verandah and closing it in, to make it into a room.

Now there was a party to celebrate. Dad had really turned it on: dozens of T-bones, and mounds of snags for the kids, and the wives were all charging around the kitchen putting mayonnaise in the coleslaw and passionfruit on the pavs. When I asked what the hell was going on, Mum just said, 'I thought you'd be tickled pink, love. Now you've got the bedroom back to yourself. And Maree can have the new little room.'

The new little room. That just happened to be my back verandah where I did my work. There was no way Mum would let me solder and do stuff in the bedroom. I might as well say goodbye to coloured glass.

I went into 'my' bedroom and refused to come out for the party.

It was the next morning, cleaning up, that I talked to Dad. Maree was still in bed of course, and Mum was at church, and Dad and I were fossicking around the yard for stray paper plates and plastic cups.

'Why,' I asked, 'when it is *me* that stayed home and didn't trouble you, why do you never do anything for me? And yet she goes off for nearly two years, and she has sex with blokes, and gets into drugs and stuff, and you give her everything. Why?'

My father was a very quiet man, a clerk on the water board who wore grey rib-knit cardigans and (before the Maree trouble) used to propagate dahlias. Very occasionally, as a way of affection, he'd call me 'Sis'. He never did that with Maree.

'Sis,' he said now as he started to dismantle the trestle tables, 'Sis, I know it seems unfair, but you have everything that I can give you, for already you have travelled far beyond me. But Maree is a child who still wants what I can give, and who will always need more than I will have.'

I thought that he had finished, because he worked in silence for a while as he concentrated on making the trestles form a tidy stack against the fence. At last he turned to me, and I noticed how pale the blue of his eyes was, as if the weeping for Maree had leeched out most of the colour. 'Do you really think,' he went on, 'that this one time away will be the end of it? No, Maree will be back and forth like a botfly. That's why I built the room, so she can come and go, down the side passage, without waking your mum. Because this will go on, Sis.' He looked me straight in the eye, almost as though committing me to something. 'She'll leave home, and come back, and leave again, and return again, but no matter what she does, I want her always to have a refuge from the storm.'

I was only sixteen at the time, so I was much less moved then by my father's words than I am now, writing this down. At the time I said, 'But what about my leadlight?'

Dad said, 'Yes, I've been thinking about that. How would you like to have the garage?'

The garage! All that space, closed in. I could build a proper workbench, store my pieces really well. 'But what about the car?'

'I can keep it on the street. Actually I've been thinking, now Maree's back and I don't have to drive around so much, I might sell it. Put the money into a couple of bank accounts, for when you and Maree leave school.'

It was as if he knew what was going to happen. Two years later, just after Maree and I did Year 12, he had a stroke and died. Mum had the house of course, and I had my half-the-car money for art school fees. Maree moved out again, spent her car money on — whatever she spends her money on. Moved back home, just as I was leaving to start my apprenticeship as a travelling restorer of old church windows. Over the next few years, as I went around the country building up my skills, Maree moved out again — back again — out again — back again — then out again to live with Brett up the coast ...

That's what Mum was on the phone about, a while ago: 'Marta, it's about Maree. She's left Brett. Reckons he's a lazy so-and-so ...'

(Talk about the pot calling the kettle black.)

'So anyway she's packed her bag — she's got no money of course — had to ring reverse charges — and she's hitching down. Oh Marta, I do worry ...'

'She'll be okay, Mum. She's done it before.'

'I know. But maybe this time ...'

'No, not this time, Mum. Nothing will happen.' (Why do I always argue when I speak with my mother?)

'Anyway the thing is, I don't know that — just at the moment — I'm quite up to it. I mean, as you know, Maree's always welcome here — of course you both are, though *you* never ... But anyway Doctor said, just last week, what with my blood pressure ...'

It went on longer than this of course, much longer than this, because we had to go back over the whole saga of Maree leaving home the first time, and why was that, and if only her father were here, and if things had been different, and (yes, I swear it!) 'Maree was always so good at poetry ...' but in the end of course I said, 'Mum, when she arrives, stick her in a taxi with just enough for her fare, and send her over to my place. She can camp here for a while.'

'Are you sure?' and 'I couldn't possibly!' and so on — we even had an argument about whether or not Mum should send some extra bedding with her, or maybe a few tins of things. 'I know how hard up you students always are.'

'Mum, I've got money! And I'm not a student — I got the St Paul's job. My first window!'

That of course passed over her — or she passed over it. 'Well, if you're sure, love ...'

'Sure I'm sure.'

I can hear the taxi outside now. Maree's laugh as she tips the driver. The slam as he gets her haversack from the boot. I look back at my phone doodle, my design for the east chapel: the arrival of the Prodigal, seen from the point of view of the jealous sibling. A load of self-indulgent shit.

Ah, but all around the border is the theme for a cheerful parable: for I have drawn, I realise, the lilies of the field, who toiled not, neither did they spin, and yet even Solomon in all his glory was not arrayed like one of these.

(Imagine the colours I'll be able to explore with this!)

The door is open. Maree comes in, her bright face bringing the sense of sunlight that always seems to shine right through her.

'Thanks, Sis,' I tell her, lifting the heavy pack off her shoulders: for extravagant as ever, she has given me my first window. A miracle in deed.

THE KNOWN SOLDIER

It was his waist she fell in love with. Not the belt, but the air inside it. So thin and empty. Vulnerable: that was the word. No it wasn't. He couldn't be vulnered ever again. But this air, this space (not *nothing*, not a vacuum like in Science) inside the belt reached out into some place inside her own inside, and she fell in love.

The belt itself was khaki, made of cotton webbing, with a rectangular buckle (a bit tarnished. She longed to polish it for him) depicting a half-sun with the rays coming out like a punk hairdo. *At the going down of the sun.* That was a bit of the poem that was in the documents Miss Hedge had made them summarise before they came to the War Memorial:

> At the going down of the sun
> And in the [something],
> We will remember them.

Below the belt was a little white card:

> Typical belt of infantryman
> Gallipoli Campaign 1915

Typical? He wasn't typical, her soldier, he was himself. How dare they?

'Alexis,' said Miss Hedge, 'move along please, quickly now. The others are already up to Flanders.'

Flanders. Flanders Field. That was in the documents too. It sounded peaceful, a green paddock full of flowers with cows chewing their way towards the creek flats. Not like Ypres, which Miss Hedge pronounced 'Wipers', harsh and spiky. In Flanders Field she found his boots.

They weren't very large and, like the buckle, needed a good polish. But even without the way the leather had gone all hard and cracked they looked as if they'd be terribly uncomfortable to walk in. No bouncing along on top of the world like Alexis in her new Nikes. She imagined his poor feet, pale and thin, with the skin gone a bit wrinkly from the perpetual seeping in of mud. She wanted to knit socks for him. He had lovely long straight toes.

At Singapore there were his pants. Far too hot for him in the heat, poor love. When Nan went to Singapore with the bowling club she just took cotton frocks and sandals. She really liked the shopping but reckoned there was never a scrap of beetroot in the salad at the hotel where they stayed, and the water pressure wasn't up to much either. Terribly muggy, Nan said, the climate over there. So why did they put him in these hot heavy pants?

Alexis's eye grazed a photograph that made her turn her head away. These men weren't wearing pants, but rags wrapped like nappies around their loins. Loins? You could hardly call them that because loins are plump like chops, and these men were made out of spaghetti. '*After the Fall of Singapore,*' said the white card, '*those taken captive were put to work on the Burma Railroad. Conditions were...*'

But he wasn't caught, he'd escaped, like Alexis, who was forging ahead now into the wild lush jungles of New Guinea.

It was steamy hot here too of course, with lots of leeches, but at least there was shade beneath the rainforest canopy. On the Kokoda Trail with the Fuzzy Wuzzy Angels he wore this shirt that was pinned out in the glass case, frail and brown as a night moth.

Alexis measured herself against the garment, or tried to, bending over the glass case, positioning her middle at the place where she thought his shirt would tuck into his pants, so that she could see where her face would be when she kissed him. And now her breast pressed on the glass and her mouth was over the little V that would be bare neck above his top button, and her breath sighed out and smudged as Miss Hedge arrived behind her, clapping her hands, demanding, 'What on earth are you doing, Alexis Carmichael?'

(Nothing on earth, Miss, nothing in earth, but in air — fire — water — those are his elements.)

And in Vietnam they'd placed his hat, just a hat ('typical' they'd probably say, in their typical way), a larrikin-slouchy digger's hat with a badge holding the brim curl, but special to her because it had once held the head, brain, mind that were his, and his alone. No one else, in the whole history of the universe, had ever had a thought that was precisely identical to any thought that had ever been inside that hat.

She had him framed now, from toe to top, through belt and buckle, boots and badge, so she could join the others who were in a pack, crowded around an archway.

Alexis, who was tall (though not as tall as he), peered over the crush and saw a hole in the floor with a little grid of mesh over it, and a flame inside. Beside it was a sheath of flowers, spiky as the name of Ypres, gasping for breath inside the cellophane. 'The tomb of the Unknown Soldier,' Miss Hedge was saying, 'mumble rhubarb.' Above, on the wall inside the arch, were names and names, names and names and names and names but not *his* name, Miss Hedge said, we do not know his name, for he is a symbolic representation of the ordinary, average, typical ...

No — Alexis protested, running fast in her Nikes past the glass cases and taking him out into the afternoon — *No, he is not typical but unique, not symbolic but real, not ordinary but quite extraordinary, and definitely not unknown, to me at least!*

It'd be ages before the others arrived so Alexis sat and waited on the step, crooking up her knees and clasping her arms around them, as if to hold him safe inside her. After a while she began to feel the last rays of the sun warm through the marble.

THE MOST UNFORGETTABLE CHARACTER I HAVE EVER MET

He was the boy next door.

Long-limbed, red-haired, with a freckled face and a larrikin grin — at the school fancy dress competition he won the Look Like Your Favourite Australian Children's Book Character competition: he went as Ginger Meggs.

Not only were we next-door neighbours, but never a day went by in which we didn't see each other. We played together, ate together, went to school together — at least for the primary years — skipped school together, had measles together, did our homework together, avoided our homework together, slept together ... In such circumstances people always say, '*We were more like twins than friends.*'

That wasn't true of course. (I wonder if it ever is?) Not only were we poles apart physically (I was small and dark) and spiritually (where he was all smiles and sunshine, I was regarded as a difficult child), but of course we lacked that basic thing which twins have: parents in common.

(I remember how I used to wish that I was the child of Doc and Birdie.)

This was the set-up:

On the corner of a cul de sac in a quietly affluent suburb, there was a large rambling house built at the turn of the century in the Federation style, with a multitude of doorways and porches, bay windows and gables, stained glass and carved fretwork. It was set in an acre of garden that was old and dark green and jungley, with a ramshackle tennis court, a shrubbery, a pergola, and a pond with a disused fountain in it, sculpted to represent a cherub boy holding his prick and pissing.

Next door was a two-storey house built in liver-coloured brick and featuring the unornamented facade popular in the immediate post-war period. Completely dominating its quarter-acre block, it loomed down upon lawn that was regularly rolled into submission; the other features of the 'garden' were a concrete driveway, a brick double garage, a rotary clothesline, an incinerator, and three small cypresses which had been topiarised into cones with a bobble on the top.

THE MOST UNFORGETTABLE CHARACTER

The first house was not just the home of my best friend but the centre of the community — insofar as there was a community in that respectable middle-class suburb. Birdie and Doc were both doctors, and they ran a busy general practice from the big old house. Cars would pull up, people would go in and ring on the side door, not just for the three appointed surgery sessions, but at any time of the morning, noon or night. So although he was an only child, there was a continual thrum of people around him — all the patients coming and going (obviously), but also Miss Sinclair, the day receptionist; Miss Elkingstone, the night receptionist; Mrs Robbo, who cleaned the surgery; Mrs Mac, who cleaned the house; Vera, who came twice a week to do the mending and ironing, and of course Birdie and Doc themselves, racing out on house calls or emergencies, racing back for surgery or a sandwich, never in the one place for longer than five seconds, and never in the same place together.

The result was that he was totally unsupervised — free would be another word for it — because every adult always thought that some other adult must be keeping an eye on him ...

My family was the opposite, but the effect was the same.

I was the youngest of seven: an Afterthought my

mother said (meaning Mistake). She'd had three wonderful sons, followed by three beautiful daughters, and that was it. But then, when the third daughter was five years old and starting school and giving my mother back the small pleasures of tennis mornings and coffee afternoons — along I came.

Oddly enough, despite the respective sizes of our families, my lot were Anglicans, and it was Doc and Birdie (christened Bridie; the nickname reflected her flamboyant plumage, her bright darting eyes) who were the Irish Catholics.

And despite the size of my family, it was always quiet and dull at my house, for my parents had the six eldest offspring organised into such a complicated roster of piano lessons, football practice, ballet rehearsals, scouts, church fellowship, maths coaching, cadets, cookery classes, choir, et cetera that my siblings were mostly out of the house doing one (or more) of these things, with my mother chauffeuring them there and my father at work to get the money to pay for it all.

Meanwhile, I ran wild with the boy next door.

Snapshot memories:

Making bows and arrows out of bamboo and being Robin Hood and Little John (no points for guessing who was leader, who was follower) under the greenwood along the driveway, until we shot the windscreen of Birdie's car instead of the Sheriff of Nottingham ...

Making the fountain in the pond work (or attempting to) by digging up the old pipes, which unfortunately turned out to be connected to the sewer line that serviced the whole street ...

Making a pirate ship out of an iron bedstead high up in the roofs; it slithered down one stormy night, smashing slates as it went ...

And then there were the less destructive things, like:

Making a crystal radio set and picking up the conversation of a Russian astronaut in a satellite, speaking in code to KGB agents who had been sent to Australia to assassinate Mr Menzies.

Making lemonade from the fruit of the old bush lemon tree and setting up a stall at the gate to flog it to the patients as they came in.

Making cigarettes out of dried lawn cuttings and mixed herbs, rolled in toilet paper, and smoking them till we went green.

Making four-decker sandwiches consisting of a layer of baked beans, a layer of peanut butter, a layer of banana, and a layer of strawberry jam.

Making cubbies in a thousand and one hidey holes around the garden, and sitting in them for hours reading comics and munching fruit cake and not doing our homework.

Making billycarts and sleds, treehouses and forts, tin canoes and oil-drum rafts, or (on wet days) model aeroplanes and balsa wood ships and mediaeval armour and ...

That's when we'd read books too.

Or rather, he would read and I would listen, for though I had no actual literacy problem, I lacked his ability to make the characters jump off the page and come alive.

So, as the rain sluiced down the window panes and cut off the world, we would curl up together in one of the many cosy nooks of that big old house, and he'd read out loud from a battered collection of books, some of which I think Doc must have had when he was a child. There were *Boy's Own Annuals* dating back through the decades, but I also remember *Winnie the Pooh*, *The Wind in the Willows*, *Tom Brown's Schooldays*, *The Adventures of Tom Sawyer* ... And as he read we would not just identify with but *become* the characters in our imaginations. Of course we particularly liked books in which there were *two* heroes, because that meant we could each have a role, as we did with Robin and Little John.

And so we would be Tom Brown and George Arthur, best chums at the English boarding school of Rugby in the 1830s. Or we'd be the other Tom and his mate Huck, hiding away on an island in the Mississippi some fifty years later. Or we'd be Ratty and Mole, mucking about in a boat on a different river; or sometimes even (I blush to admit) those soppy stuffed toys, Pooh and Piglet, walking arm-in-arm through the snow of a nursery woodland.

If all this itself sounds like something from an outdated children's book, I should perhaps explain in our defence that we were born before television came to Australia, and though it arrived when we were five, our respective families did not buy their sets until we were in our early teens, so that our enthusiasm for all these old-fashioned pastimes was not out of innocence, but simply because we had the time to play.

No, we certainly weren't innocent. How could we be, when we had the surgery to explore?

It was the only part of that whole acre of paradise that was out of bounds; which of course only made it more enticing.

And just as Adam and Eve must have savoured the act of slowly circling the Tree of Knowledge of Good and Evil, sniffing and selecting the forbidden fruit, there were also layers or levels of sin that we could progress through before we reached the holy of holies.

First there was the porch, where the patients would deposit wet umbrellas and laden shopping trolleys, leave the occasional bicycle or tie up a dog. It was somehow fascinating to poke around there.

While this bit of stickybeaking had to be done during surgery hours, the inner circles could only be penetrated during the two-hour intervals that occurred between morning surgery and afternoon surgery and afternoon surgery and evening surgery; or on Sunday afternoons, which was the only time that both doctors took off.

In those days there was no thought of locking doctors' surgeries to prevent drug thefts, so we would simply glance around to make sure the coast was clear, and then slip through the porch door and into the waiting room with its comfy sagging chairs, its aquarium of goldfish, its crate of jigsaws and alphabet blocks, its stack of dog-eared magazines including our beloved *Reader's Digests* (of which more later). It would have been possible to spend the whole day mucking about in the waiting room.

But next there was the desk, with its internal as well as external telephones (a real novelty in those days), and its great array of office gadgetry — In trays and Out trays and pen stands and pencil holders and containers for paperclips and containers for drawing pins and containers for butterfly clips and containers to put containers in. You could play Receptionist there, taking appointments over the internal phone for rude ailments suffered by people like the school principal, Her Majesty the Queen, Donald Duck, the Pope, and my three sisters. Or you could just fiddle about in the little containers.

Behind that was the office, where stationery of all kinds was stacked in shelves: typing paper (foolscap and quarto), index cards, memo pads, blotter pads and jotter pads, account pads, prescription pads (our favourite of course: we'd write scrips for our enemies — recommending five spoonfuls of bat's blood to be taken three times daily — or for ourselves, calling for a lamington and a bottle of Coke before meals), and filing cabinets containing the patients' records (which were the only things that didn't interest us at all of course: we were too egoistical to wish to read about other people).

Adjoining the office was the toilet (just a normal toilet, but very useful when the excitement would threaten an accident) and the washroom, with a sink as well as hand basin to splash around in, and the steriliser unit winking its red light.

All of this however was still just a warm-up, a dalliance, a mere flirtation ...

There were two consulting rooms of course, one for Doc and one for Birdie. His had maroon leather chairs and black and white prints depicting funny characters from the novels of Charles Dickens; her furniture had bright canvas slip covers — deep pink and verdant green, acid yellow and peacock blue — and on the walls were prints of Rousseau's jungle paintings.

Now that you'd reached this stage, you could each sit in a consulting room, behind a desk, and talk to imaginary patients for a while; but when that began to pall you could take turns being doctor and patient, one of you behind the desk, the other in the second chair. Of course, the next step was ...

The examination room.

This was a small room with no windows and a high leather couch which was always covered with a scrupulously clean white sheet. There was a smell in here, of floor wax and antiseptic, leather and starch; and a sense of nakedness of course, nudity, bodies; and an atmosphere that somehow made you think of poking and prodding and looking ...

At this stage, greatly daring, the patient one of us would clamber up onto the couch; ease down pants, then underpants; lie face up, then face down; and the doctor one of us would do things.

A different but somehow equally sensual thrill was

provided by opening the cupboard at the end of this annexe and simply looking at the array of sterilised forceps and scalpels, tweezers and probes. The kidney-shaped enamel bowls, even the bags of swabs and dressing strips, not to mention the syringes, could make the inside of your stomach quiver with a strange cold queasiness.

Or perhaps it was just the fear of being caught that turned us on.

After this, if our nerves could stand it, we would Open the Drawer. Part of the wooden framework of the examination couch, this must have been intended as a storage place for instruments, but Doc and Birdie used it as a hidey hole for the sorts of things that were scandalous in the 1950s: packets of condoms, tubes of spermicidal jelly, diaphragms, douches, and a few selected texts such as *Studies in the Psychology of Sex*, by Havelock Ellis; a first edition of the *Kinsey Report*; 'Growing Up', produced by the Father & Son Association; and Marie Stopes's *Married Love*. This drawer was fitted with a brass lock, but we knew where the key was kept: on top of the door lintel.

Looking back, I wonder if this locked drawer was meant to keep things from the prying eyes of children and cleaning ladies, or from the omniscience of God Himself; for Birdie and Doc, as I have said, were

Catholics, though obviously humane ones.

When it all became too much we would lock the drawer, shut the cupboard door, straighten the sheet on the couch, and run back to the waiting room, where my friend would read me excerpts from *Reader's Digest*. Somehow we needed this innocuous winding down time before we could go outside again and turn back into Robin Hood and Little John.

We loved all the joke sections and little features in the *Digest*, from 'Laughter, the Best Medicine' to 'Humour in Uniform', but we gained our greatest glee from the anecdotes entitled 'The Most Unforgettable Character I Have Ever Met'. These were folksy, sentimental vignettes of the kind that only Americans could produce, and were supposedly sent in by rank and file readers as warm and genuine as apple pie. Yet though the by-lines were always different, and the 'Characters' varied from 'My Army Sergeant' to 'My Grade School Teacher', 'The Local Chief of Police' to 'The Local Preacher', they were somehow always exactly the same: I guess that was their attraction. Like episodes of TV soapies, or loaves of sliced white bread, it was the combination of predictability and lack of substance that enabled them to fill a need, for after Marie Stopes we just weren't up to anything stronger — or stranger.

THE MOST UNFORGETTABLE CHARACTER

After reading two or three 'Characters' each, we would have giggled ourselves sober, and would be able to sneak out through the porch into the sunshine again.

Of course all these games went on when we were still primary kids, attending the state school half a mile away from home. That's when we were truly inseparable, walking to school together every day, walking home together, sitting together in class, often having breakfast together, often eating tea together, often sleeping over at each other's places.

At the end of sixth class the first break happened. I was sent to an Anglican school; he of course went to a Catholic one, run by a certain order of brothers.

'What are they like?' I used to ask at first. As a Protestant of the 1950s I was morbidly fascinated by priests, brothers, men who wore long robes and made vows not to get married ...

'Do they really never get married?' I asked.

'Course not,' he said.

'How weird,' I scoffed, expecting him to join in.

'Not really,' he said in a quiet sort of voice. Then added: 'I don't expect I shall.'

Despite the books in the locked drawer I was still pretty dim about what marriage entailed, but that struck me as just about the oddest thing I'd ever heard.

In the 1950s, grown-up people automatically got married, just as husbands went off to work and women stayed home and the moon went round the earth and so on. To say that you didn't expect to get married was like saying you didn't expect to get a job: unthinkable.

'*How come?*' I spluttered in disbelief.

'Oh, Peter — I dunno,' he shrugged. 'I guess I just don't feel like it.'

As if I'd asked him to do something both unimportant and immediate, like go for a bike ride or make a four-decker sandwich or play the latest hit record by Col Joye and the Joy Boys.

He looked at me gravely, considering, and then abruptly focused away from me, into the far distance.

Did I happen to mention his eyes? Green, sea-green you'd have to say, for at times they were blue, and at other times gold flecks seemed to wash through them like shifting sands. He would use them for punctuation and gesture, as some European people use their hands, and he had a strange knack of catching and holding the eye of whomever he was speaking to, if he really wished them to listen.

The change to secondary school didn't just mean that we were now apart for all the hours of the day swallowed up by going to school, being at school, coming home from school; the nature of secondary school in itself allowed the chalk-and-cheeseness of our different personalities to emerge. So when it came to choosing subjects, I selected Chemistry, Physics, Maths I, Maths II, Biology and English. He selected English, Art, Ancient History, Modern History, Biology and General Maths. With his long limbs and easy grace he was a natural athlete; my shortness, together with a lack of physical co-ordination, made me a dud at any sport.

But though we were unable now to share the experience (for better or worse) of school, on every weekday we would still make the opportunity to go through the fence and see each other if only for half an hour or so, and we would spend the whole of the weekend together, except for the time that was taken up by his sporting activities. School holidays were still our best times, when day after day we would be in each other's company and when we'd still mostly spend the night together, staying usually at his place but sometimes at mine.

Of course by now we didn't get up to pranks. As befitted our new roles as teenagers we lolled about listening to the hit parade on our transistors, or indeed (for our parents had now bought television sets) *watching* shows like *Bandstand* and *6 O'clock Rock*.

As to the whole surgery business and what we used to do in there, we somehow just stopped, without discussing it or ever mentioning it again. It was as if all that had never happened.

But it had.

And in that game alone, it was I who had been the leader.

If starting high school is a rite of passage that often separates childhood friends, another one is provided by the physical onset of puberty. How often do you see a couple of kids — whether boys or girls — who muck around together till they're eleven or twelve or so, then suddenly one shoots up — or out — and gets pimples and discovers sex, while the other is a sort of Rip Van Winkle for a few years, sleeping in a prepubescent state; and the whole basis of friendship between the two is broken? You'll see them pass each other in the street, barely speaking. The older one will despise the younger one as a dag. And the younger one will hate the older one simply for growing.

That old/young division happened with us of course. And again there are no points for guessing who was leader, by a long shot. He was six foot tall with a properly modulated voice and a full quota of pubic hair when I was barely out of short pants, with so few hairs that I could count them, and still squawking like Tiny Tim.

But with us it made no difference.

At school, I'd feel so inadequate when the other blokes would pass around copies of *Man* magazine, when they'd talk about how they'd done it to Janice Roylance who was supposedly the bike from the nearby high school, or simply when they'd flaunt their size around the change rooms after swimming lessons. It was just as bad with the less macho ones, who would gossip about which of the Presbyterian Ladies College girls might be on the train that afternoon, and what to say to them, and how to ask them to the movies.

But he never did that kind of stuff. He never left me out, or put me down.

And so we went on.

At last it was time for us to do our final year of school, make our plans for university. There was no question as to our going there — all moderately intelligent middle class children simply did, in those days. Nor was there much question as to what we'd study: Arts for him, Medicine for me.

(Did I ever consciously wonder why I chose that? When I chose? Looking back, I wonder if it was because of the special fascination that the surgery had always had for me; or whether the motivation wasn't to do with the broader fascination of every single thing about his life, his house, his parents ... If I couldn't have Doc and Birdie as my father and mother, then I could become a doctor myself, and try to live a facsimile of their lives. Was that it? And in turn, did I want them as my parents, so I could *be* him?)

Anyway, we filled out our enrolment forms, did our exams, got our results, and then settled in for the long wait till uni would start in March. For me, there was a double sense of change coming, because I would be leaving home then too: my parents had insisted on booking me into the Anglican men's college at the university, where my brothers had all resided during their uni time. My sense of anticipation about this was not lessened by the fact that I did not want to go — for the simple reason that he would not be there. ('Never mind, Pete,' he'd try to cheer me up. 'I'll come and visit. Sleep on your floor.' And we swore that we'd have lunch together every day, and go to the pub together after lectures.)

Long summer holidays were of course always heaven for him and me, but this time it was a particularly hot February and the bliss was going on a bit too long. By now he had his driver's licence and he would nag Birdie for a loan of her car for a couple of hours so we could go to the beach or even just the pool in the next suburb. We were constantly late getting the car back, which made her late for her house calls, so on the Monday morning of the last week she yelled, '*Enough!*' With her swift efficiency she got on the phone and rang an old friend whose husband had a fishing hideaway on a river about five hours up the coast, then she rang Avis and rented herself a car for the week, gave us her car and a list of directions for finding the shack and a considerable number (for those days) of twenty dollar notes, and shoved us out the door. 'I don't want to see you two back here till Sunday!' she threatened.

I realise that I have used the words 'heaven', 'paradise' and so on quite often here, so that there is no expression left for that hideaway on the river. But try to imagine:

You head north for a few hours, and at a certain point between two small towns you branch off the highway towards the coast. After twenty kilometres or so you discover a cluster of houses, a general store, and a pub with a wide verandah that overlooks the broad estuary of a tidal river. You park the car, and if you walk for a few minutes towards the east you reach a long stretch of deserted beach, with the breakers rolling in an even progression. Or you can load the car with groceries, sausages, ice for the esky, a bag of bait, a few bottles of beer, and drive west along a sandy track that follows the course of the river, winding through scrub first and then forest, to take you to a little clearing. Here you leave the car, load yourself up with your luggage, and hike along a foot track for ten minutes or so until you reach an old green corrugated iron boatshed that juts from the bank out across the edge of the water. You go in, to find that the shed contains — as well as dinghy and oars — a primus stove and a kerosine lamp and just the right amount of frying pans and billies and mugs and stuff, and even things that you've forgotten like salt and zinc cream, peanut butter and a tin of chocolate biscuits. Above you, slats of wood have been criss-crossed over the rafters to make a sleeping loft which you reach by a rope ladder; up here is a double mattress, inside a pure white tent of mosquito net; there is even a little round clerestory window, to allow the full moon to peep at you.

If years before we had imagined ourselves as a couple of happy-go-lucky river dwellers through the characters of Ratty and Mole, or Tom Sawyer and Huck Finn, now we had a chance to play with a real river. So absorbed were we in the discovery of the joys of mucking about in a boat that mornings, afternoons, whole days would drift into a golden shimmer like the light along the bank at dawn. We'd eat when we were hungry, fall asleep when we were tired, slip into and out of the water, maybe dangle a line, pull in a fish, light a fire, eat again ...

Every couple of days we'd drive or even row down to the little settlement, have a surf, replenish our supplies, and then return to (I have to use the word) our Eden.

Before we knew it, it was Saturday. Our last surf. Our last visit to the general store — just for milk and bread; no point buying ice — we'd be going tomorrow.

And because we had no ice, we went into the pub for a drink instead of simply taking a couple of bottles home.

There was a pool table, and after the second beer we put our money in the slot, set up the balls, and were about to start when a couple of blokes came up to us. They had bike leathers on, tattoos, asked if we wanted to play doubles.

'Fine by us ...' We could hardly say 'No'.

'Let's make it more interesting, eh?' one of them suggested, putting a dollar note on the table.

'Okay,' we said again.

They were hustling us of course, and we must have looked like easy marks — nice little private school boys that we were — but my father had a billiard table, so we'd had quite a lot of practice over the years. They let us win at first — or thought they were letting us win, but we too were playing well below our abilities — and they naturally kept raising the size of the bet. When it came to the climax, when there was real money on the table and they were ready to play properly, we played properly too. And it was us who won it.

Suddenly I realised that they weren't intending to give us the money, and indeed I wondered if we weren't going to get our heads punched in as well. But then the publican intervened. He was an old mate of Birdie's friend's husband — we'd introduced ourselves as soon as we'd arrived in town — and now he told the two blokes to give us the cash, and if there was any trouble — outside or anywhere — they'd be barred from the pub for life.

They swore and reckoned that was all their money for petrol for the weekend; but they were just a couple of local bikeriders and not (as I'd thought) the leaders of a chapter of the Hell's Angels, so they did as they were told.

Outside though, as we were getting into the car, one of them approached us and held out his fist.

Here we go, I thought.

But he had a little plastic bag instead of a knuckleduster. Would we like to buy this with the money we'd just won from them?

Too right we would.

THE MOST UNFORGETTABLE CHARACTER

Not only had we never tried it (well, I hadn't), but to buy it would clearly provide a solution to the problems of petrol and honour, and would make it less likely that they would follow us home and punch our heads in (I hoped).

Back at the boatshed, dangling our legs over the edge and watching the night settle along the river, he started to laugh. 'It'll only be dried lawn cuttings and mixed herbs, you know. They just hustled us again.'

But for once he was wrong.

It was only leaf, no heads or anything, but that's enough, when it's the first time, to make an impression. The night became very mellow and after a while we cooked up all the leftovers into the most wonderful concoction, which we ate in the darkness. Had a cup of tea. Another smoke. Watched the moonbeams snag on the ripples. Time flowed past too, and after a while we found ourselves reminiscing about our primary school days, the teachers we'd had, the kids we'd known.

Suddenly I found myself relating a piece of gossip I'd heard recently about a boy called Stretch Carter, who'd been the blockhead of our Grade 6 class. The latest story was, he'd got some girl pregnant because he'd thought that a reliable method of contraception was to dunk your balls in a glass of cold water beforehand.

I'd expected a response as uproarious and immature as my own (I am ashamed to say I didn't even think of the poor girl's situation), but all I got was a polite smile. 'Well, at least that's one thing I don't have to worry about,' he murmured.

Huh?

'I'm queer,' he added in a matter of fact voice.

For the last twenty years or so, 'queer' has been a wrong word (though I notice it's coming into fashion again; there's a Queer Literature conference in town this weekend, I see from today's newspaper) but this was February 1968, before the new meaning of the word 'gay', let alone the Gay Liberation Movement, arrived in Australia. (Just as we had pre-dated television, we were a bit too early for the revolution.) Anyway, whatever the politics of the word, I simply did not know what he meant.

My mother used to say 'queer' as an alternative to 'collywobbles in the tummy'. 'Are you feeling queer, dear?' she'd say during long drives to my second sister, who suffered from car sickness. 'Tell me if you need the bucket.'

So when he told me he was queer I thought he meant that the weird and wonderful leftover stew had been too much for him.

'Well, just chuck over the edge,' I suggested.

'You don't even know what I'm talking about, do you?' he sighed, and then he told me in more detail. He hadn't actually done it yet, not *with* anyone, but he knew, he'd always known, he said.

I was out of my depth. Though I had learnt to grunt and giggle over magazines with the other boys at school, sexuality (of whichever variety) was still completely beyond my personal experience, just as Beethoven's Fifth is outside the world of a deaf person. But that didn't make his revelation any better: quite the opposite.

Well, that's my defence for what I did — and didn't do.

Actually, at first I did nothing.

Said nothing.

Nothing at all.

After a long time, he shrugged and muttered, 'Anyway, I'm going to bed.' Then — obviously realising the implications that word now had — he blurted, 'Don't worry, I won't rape you or anything.' He rose and headed for the rope ladder; when he was halfway up he added, 'If it's any consolation, I don't even happen to fancy you. I guess you're too much like my twin, or something.'

That was no consolation at all.

I was —

(By now a delayed reaction had set in, but what exactly was I feeling? Shock? Outrage? Devastation? Yes, all that, and more. After so many years, I still cannot find the word for it. I was also of course stoned — for the first time in my life — and I must have drunk at least half a dozen beers during that pool game. So that I was probably moving back and forth through a variety of responses, not least of which would have been the generalised paranoia which marijuana tends to bring.)

I would sleep where I was, downstairs, I decided, but after an hour or more the mozzies were too bad so I found myself following him up to the loft.

I wonder now: were the mosquitoes just an alibi, an excuse? Did I follow him up to bed in the hope that he *would* make an approach to me? I don't think so. Perhaps I simply sought the reassurance of sleeping next to him as I had ever since I could remember.

It was hot of course in that loft, beneath the tin roof, and every other night of this week I had slept in my underpants, as he had. Tonight I left on t-shirt, jeans, even my belt.

When the moon came out from behind a cloud I saw that he too was fully dressed. He was lying there, still as still, in an unnaturally tidy position on his own half of the mattress, with his arms at his sides. His eyes were closed, and for the first time I noticed how long his lashes were.

I lay down on my half of the mattress, tucked the mosquito net under so that we were both safe inside our white transparent cubby.

I could feel the space of air that divided us as palpably as if it had been a bolster.

Did he sleep a wink?

I certainly did not.

At the first glimmer of dawn I rose as quietly as I could, made my way down the ladder, to the door, which I opened ...

What made me turn back?

What monstrous, mean, small, spiteful devil made me turn back and pocket the little bag of dope before returning to the door, going out onto the track, walking to the settlement, catching a lift on the milk truck to the highway, and then hitching home to my own house where I went into my bedroom and packed my belongings and did not come out until it was time for my father to drive me to the residential college, the next day?

I betrayed him twice more, after that.

I mean that there were two more occasions on which I deliberately turned my back on him, as well as all the other occasions which I could have taken to search him out, see him, apologise.

As to these sins of omission, it was very easy to avoid him at university, for the Medical Faculty was situated near the colleges, down past the ovals, while his subjects of English and Government and Fine Arts were over the other side of the campus. For a while I ran the risk of seeing him if I went home to have a meal, get my washing done, but soon he also moved out, to a squat in the suburb next to the university (his parents told my parents).

But if I didn't see him in real life, I saw his photo often enough in the student newspaper — burning his draft card, getting arrested — and then articles by him and even short bits of fiction began to appear too.

I was busy myself of course, for the act of living in a men's college brought a number of time-consuming occupations: such as getting drunk most nights of the week, and going on raids at the nearby women's college, and committing sadistic pranks upon blokes who were seen as wimps. The fact that I myself was small and basically wimpy meant of course that I had to take part in what we called 'animal acts' with the fervour of a fanatic — or else it would have been me who was driven to the outskirts of the city and left to find my own way back to college, wearing nothing but a blindfold. And as well as all this there were lectures and pracs, dragging on for six years, and then more study when I decided to specialise as a psychiatrist.

When was it that the Gay Liberation marches and protests started?

I don't know, but I do know that one of the early demonstrations coincided with our college Foundation Day, an occasion that we college men celebrated by going on a pub crawl.

And the last of the pubs that we crawled into was the very pub where he and half a dozen of his co-demonstrators were putting aside their Gay Rights placards and having a quiet ale.

I was actually standing next to him at the bar when I became aware of him. The barmaid put two beers down on the counter; he passed one to a boy with curly blond hair at the table behind us, then turned and grinned at me as if we were as friendly as ever. 'What're *you* having?' he asked, adding another dollar to the money he was holding ready for the barmaid.

'I'm already in a shout,' I snarled, then — terrified in case any of my mates had seen me even speaking to someone wearing a Gay Lib t-shirt — I raced away from the bar, out of the pub, back to college, where I lay on my bed and retched into the wastepaper basket for twenty-four hours. It was as if I was trying to empty myself out of my body in the way that one simply empties the vacuum cleaner of its accumulation of grunge.

Looking back, I try to understand the primary cause of this self-disgust. Was it, for example, based more on the dope theft than the memories of the examination room? Or is that just wishful thinking?

Put it another way: perhaps instead of asking why I turned back at the boatshed to take the dope, I should be inquiring as to why I was leaving?

Of course, there can be no simple answer, for the very fact that I am in a position to *look back* means that I am distanced from the person I was then. I mean: not only have I myself changed in two and a half decades, but so have social attitudes to homosexuality — or at least amongst the circles I move in. And if 'gay' is now a shorthand way of saying something, so is 'homophobia' a quick way to describe the fear of homosexuality (usually based of course on the homophobe's own unrecognised homosexual feelings).

But is that what I was suffering from?

Or was it just a rather ordinary case of unrequited love?

Physician, heal thyself!

THE MOST UNFORGETTABLE CHARACTER

His name came up of course when my parents were making the list for invitations to my wedding. They'd moved house by now, to somewhere smaller, but still exchanged Christmas cards with their old neighbours Doc and Birdie, whose names were automatically put on the list, along with his.

I crossed it off.

My mother raised her eyebrows at me.

'You wouldn't like him these days — he's a Communist,' I said. 'He went in those anti-Vietnam moratorium things.'

'Oh well then ...' my mother agreed, and nothing more was said.

Doc and Birdie, as it turned out, were unable to come.

But to my amazement, when the Best Man read out the telegrams, there was one addressed *to the Most Unforgettable Character I Have Ever Met.*

'Lots of Luck,' it said, which the Best Man (who was pissed as a newt) first read as 'Lots of Love'.

It wasn't signed.

That was the last I heard of him until this morning when, opening the newspaper, I saw his name among a list of speakers who would be giving papers at the Queer Lit conference this weekend. There was a brief biographical note about him, saying that although Aus-

tralian-born, he is best known in England, where he has made his home now for the last couple of decades and is highly regarded both as an activist and theoretician ...
I go of course.

It is meant to be one of my weekends for access but my fifteen-year-old daughter has decided she'd rather spend the time with her boyfriend, so what else have I to do? Besides, the registration fee is tax deductible, for I have a number of gay patients and of course a lot of my time is spent helping them examine their childhoods. (If only it were so easy to make sense of one's own.)

He is giving the paper at the afternoon session, on (the program states) 'The Homosexual Couple in Children's Literature'.

I watch him up on the platform as someone or other introduces him.

He hasn't changed at all. Red hair keeps its colour well, and that long lanky sort of frame doesn't run to fat.

Whereas my own hair is pretty much a thing of the past, and the years of too much lunch have turned my short body into a barrel. What with my thick horn-rimmed specs, the overall impression is of a bald-headed owl.

He starts to speak, and I must admit that for quite

some time I am totally absorbed by the sound rather than meaning of his words. His middle-class Australian speech has been overlaid with an English accent — not that awful BBC stuff, but something attractive like the cockney on that *EastEnders* TV show. Yet if the sound of his talking has changed, his method of delivery is the same — so that he still uses his eyes for emphasis, looking down from the platform and catching the eye of every single member of the audience simultaneously. Or that's how it seems. (You could hear a pin drop.)

When at last I tune in to the words, he is saying that by and large children's book writers seem to feel comfortable about depicting a homosexual couple living happily in some prepubescent Garden of Eden. 'Indeed,' he declares, 'gay couples are the *heroes* in a number of the classics of children's literature.' He gives examples:

Tom Brown and George Arthur.

Huck Finn and Tom Sawyer.

Pooh and Piglet. (The audience giggles.)

Ratty and Mole. ('Now *there* was a couple of happy old bachelors!')

'However,' he goes on to say, 'when the scene changes from one of these innocent Edens to a representation of contemporary real life, and when both the characters and the audience become old enough to realise their homosexuality and do something *with* it ...' He pauses and grins cheekily down from the platform, before continuing: 'We find again and again that at this stage of the story, the writer will deliberately break the relationship — by sending one of the characters into exile, or even by killing one of the characters — in order to avoid seeming to say that gay people can be happy and have successful and lasting relationships.'

He names various young adult books in which this happens, but they're unfamiliar to me, and anyway I find myself drifting into thought.

At the end of his session, a number of members of the audience mill up to the podium, ask him to sign books that they've brought along (I didn't know he'd written books!), or just their program.

I hang back in my seat.

After a while I hear him suggest to the last handful of fans that they continue this interesting discussion in the pub.

Keeping a few metres distance I follow the group to the hotel on the corner, which is full of the overflow from the conference. These are gay men, gay women, gay young adults of all shapes and sizes and ages and colours and fashion styles but amongst them all I feel conspicuous.

And then, even worse, I feel inconspicuous.

I feel invisible.

I realise that I am the only person in this crowded pub no one is talking to, or even noticing.

I go up to the bar, gently squeeze into a space that will allow me to order, for I feel that if I act like everyone else I will blend in. After all, it is very dark in here.

But that turns out to be impossible. I wait and wait. No one serves me. After a long while I understand what the problem is. The three barmen are gay, and they simply do not see me.

This is like some kind of nightmare, in which one joins the walking dead and is sentenced to roam the earth eternally, unseen. A loneliness overtakes me, as it did that night in the boatshed when I realised that he had moved into a world that I could never enter, and left me outside.

After a long time, as the people being served around me get their drinks and go, and others come, and go, I hear someone at my side tell the barman: 'No, he was here before me, serve him first.' It is a slightly cockney accent, and I am aware of the tallness beside me as I turn, and we are crammed so close together that I am almost in his arms.

'Hi,' I say, 'hello.'

He smiles politely. 'Did we meet before?' he asks. 'You must forgive me. I get introduced to so many people at this sort of conference, and to tell you the truth I'm still a bit jet-lagged. I only flew in last night.'

'Sorry,' I say, 'I'm sorry.'

But he thinks I think I've trodden on his foot or something. 'It's terribly crowded, isn't it?' he grins. 'Great turn-up.'

I look into his eyes as he looks into mine, and I see no flicker of recognition there. I realise he thinks I am trying to pick him up. Even worse, I realise he is, in the kindest possible fashion, giving me the knock-back.

In my seething mind this somehow links with the literary theory he stated, and I want to grab hold of him and shout: *'Here I am! I'm the character who has been sent into exile — I'm the one who's been killed off! I know what you mean about being unhappy! But I'm the straight one!'*

Instead I push my way out into the night, which floods with images of him.

This is where the story starts.

He was the boy next door ...

(If only I could stop remembering.)

PASTORAL

Uncle Clem was a man in blue football shorts and a blue singlet. The soles of his feet were made of calluses and he seemed to walk on little springs. Onto his porridge he piled salt, spoonful after spoonful. Every morning just before dawn he ricocheted across the paddocks to get the cows up. Sometimes from her bed on the verandah Denzil could hear him yelling at Kylie, the blue cattle dog.

'Gerron, gitoutathat, gitback Kylie! One fine day, girl, you'll push a man too flaming far!'

One of the cows was red and temperamental. She was called Billy and she gave thin milk. The other forty-eight were all calm, well brought up Jerseys. Their hides were the colour of Auntie Mim's coffee, and their milk was almost pure cream. As a city child used to bottle stuff, Denzil was only able to swallow Billy's produce.

No matter how cold the morning, Uncle Clem wouldn't wear a coat. Even in winter he strode out on his bare feet through the wet grass wearing only his singlet and shorts. The singlets had originally been white but they had been pulped around in the copper with the shorts for so many years that both were now the same shade of faded iodine. Denzil liked to stand over the steaming copper in the foggy wash-shed and watch the dye seep out of the shorts and into the singlets. She would sometimes drop a handkerchief onto the top of the boiling blue water, watch it puff up into a big white bubble, and then go flat like a sigh. The blue would creep in from the edges till all the white was gone, then Denzil would fish the hanky out with the long smooth copper stick and run it under the tap or else Auntie Mim would rouse on her for spoiling it. Denzil believed that hankies were meant to be spoiled; and anyway, she had about a thousand of them. Since Denzil's mother had died, all the aunts ever gave her were hankies — or pink embroidered bags to put hankies in. Once a handkerchief had been in the copper with the shorts it always remained faintly tinged with blue.

Sometimes when Denzil was in the wash-shed Kylie would come in and push her head against the back of Denzil's knee, and Denzil would crouch down and stroke her ears and whisper, *'Good dog, Kylie, good girl, good girl.'* Denzil was on Kylie's side and liked to believe that Kylie was on hers. Everyone else had it in for Kylie because of the way she hurried the cows.

When you herd cows (Uncle Clem told Denzil) you have to do it slowly because if they run, their milk dries up. But Kylie hated the way a cow would move one foot; and another; and a third foot. Then there'd be the wait while the cow rolled down her head to the grass. Finally bite; look up; down to conclude the bite; up again; swing the head. The cow would chew like one of the aunts selecting curtain material. And then the last leg would move. It could take an hour to shift the cows from the river flat up to the bails.

And so Kylie would crouch belly-flat in a clump of grass, her long nose a fraction above the earth and swivelling back and forth like a snake, would choose a victim, take a flying leap at one of those heels, and yapyap it into life.

'Gerron, gitoutathat, gitback Kylie! One day, girl, you'll push a man too far!'

But at least one Jersey would be jogging up the slope, those fat udders swinging slap and slap against the back legs, her face a little less like Auntie Gwen's. Kylie of course never went for Billy.

When Kylie overdid it and got all the cows on the

run, Uncle Clem would lash out at her with a loop of fencing wire or a bit of wood or anything handy. Sometimes he even collected her hard in the side with his boot. Still, it was worth it, Kylie thought. Or Denzil thought Kylie thought, which was the same thing.

Willowglen ran from the road up half a mile or so of track to the house, and then down again the same distance to the river flats. On the eastern side, past the bails, it dropped through the bull paddock to the darkness of the billabong where eels lurked beneath a thick skin of algae; the fourth side just sort of dwindled away into a scrubby gully that acted as the boundary with O'Reillys. (As their name proved, they were tykes, so the natural barrier was just as well. Uncle Clem of course was Methodist. Not that he ever went to church; but when he played euchre, it was only for matches.)

With its soft pastures, its fat cows, and the long pastel green skirts of the willows that danced along the meandering river bed, the place could almost be mistaken for a farm in one of Denzil's English picture books. If she dug her fingers into the soil, however, she found warm red earth, and if she looked up, she saw the tropical green of the banana trees that clung perilously to the steep hills that enclosed the whole valley.

Like all the farms along this road, *Willowglen* was too

small to make a living from, so Uncle Clem rented one of these banana plantations. He called it his second hat. That year when the picking started, Denzil stuffed herself with the sappy unripe fruit till her belly swelled right up and she rolled on the shed floor screaming.

'Yous kids never learn!' Uncle Clem told her.

It was of course not possible to wait till the bananas ripened and eat them without agony, because all the fruit was packed green (after being dipped in a bath of sticky black stuff) and shipped away to the city. You couldn't, after all, eat the profits. (Or even, in Uncle Clem's case, the losses.)

If you could stop yourself from getting a bellyache, picking season was exciting, not least because it meant that a whole lot of new people came to the valley. The men walked up and down the rows with machetes, slashing down the bunches, and the women packed like fury, layering the bananas up and down the boxes in a herringbone pattern. That was the first time Denzil met Italians, and Yugoslavs, and Chinese, and Aborigines. There were babies and kids and dogs and old cars and the radio played all day and everyone sang along to it. The inside of the packing shed was dark, with an occasional sunspot like a gold coin where the light pierced through a nail hole in the corrugated iron roof.

One day, a hole appeared in the fibro wall of the shed

itself. Denzil saw how it happened.

It was Uncle Clem's turn to stand at the bottom of the flying fox that whizzed the huge bunches from the top of the plantation down to the shed. The trick was to throw a hessian sack over the singing wire with one hand, and hold it still for a moment, while with the other hand you grabbed off the steel hook with its catch of bananas. This time however, Denzil's uncle must have been distracted by something because when the bunch came he was just a split second too slow with the sack, so that he took with the fruit the full momentum of the flying fox and was cannoned straight into the fibro shed wall.

A couple of the women screamed, and then everyone was silent. Denzil clamped her mouth shut too. Meanwhile the bunches kept coming down and mounting up on the turning pole of the flying fox, so after a few moments Uncle Clem just picked up his body and put it back to work. You couldn't let the fruit spoil. But ever after that, the shed had an Uncle-Clem-shaped hole like a shadow puppet.

The greyhounds were the other gamble against disaster. They lived with Neil and Sue across the road. Every couple of weeks they were loaded into the station wagon and taken to the Grafton races, where usually they would win just enough to fuel both the car and the belief that one day they'd really come good. Denzil loved them too, though she couldn't identify with them as she could with Kylie.

One night after six Saturdays of losses Uncle Clem kept everyone waiting for hours while he drank in the striped tent. Auntie Mim gave Denzil her cardigan but she still shivered in the back of the station wagon with the sleeping dogs while she heard Uncle Clem's voice swearing and saying he'd sell the bludgers; and at the end of that week he did. After that, Denzil feared for Kylie.

Despite Uncle Clem, Denzil would find herself drawn each morning from her verandah bed when the level of the light showed that milking was about to start. She'd put on thick socks and gumboots, for though it was too early for snakes the paddocks were cold and wet with dew. Denzil's footprints would leave an explorer trail from the house down to the bails.

Once there, Denzil would sit on the top rail of the yard and watch as Uncle Clem or Neil would slip the four metal tubes of a milking machine on to a cow's udders and the milk would pulse down a long plastic coil while the cow kept her head in the trough and ate. When a cow was empty she was shoved out of her stall and the next one was stuck in; tubes were reconnected and another mouth chewed. Unless of course the next cow happened to be Billy: in which case Neil or Uncle Clem would shout and Kylie would bark and Billy would butt and kick and bellow and Denzil would thrill with excitement. When at last the metal was gripped on, Billy's udders would release the milk in arhythmical sputters and it would be so thin it would look palish-blue, like Denzil's hankies. Sometimes they had to milk Billy manually; on those occasions they tied one of her back legs. That winter when she went dry they slaughtered her, and after that Denzil had to mix water into milk to make it thin enough to swallow. She felt like a traitor, even touching the smug milk of those Jerseys, but somehow she had to get down the great bowl of thick salty porridge that boiled in the pan like the exploding mud rivers in Walt Disney's *The Living Desert*. If she didn't eat her porridge for breakfast, Uncle Clem made Auntie Mim keep it for her lunch. And if she didn't eat it at lunchtime, it came back again for tea.

At the end of milking, the yard steamed with fresh dung and the floor of the separator room was a creamy delta. The men would sluice out the bails with hoses and load the big cans onto the ute so they could be taken down to the little shed on the roadside. It was Denzil's job to get the milk for the house before it all went away to the city.

'Auntie Mim says only half a billy today, thanks Uncle Clem.' She always felt as if she was interrupting.

'Which half do you want — the top half or the bottom half?'

Uncle Clem cracked jokes like that, that Denzil couldn't answer. She sometimes heard him telling Neil that she was useless.

An hour later the Co-op truck would pick up the milk cans and take them into town. It would also pick up Denzil and take her to school, unless Denzil was game enough to delay on the porridge and miss the truck. Then she was safe for the day, because no one had time to drive her and unlike the other kids she didn't have a bike. But gagging on the porridge made Uncle Clem think she was useless, so staying home was only slightly better than going to school.

The school had been founded in 1892 by Denzil's grandmother, and Denzil hated it. There were camphor laurel trees all around it, and tadpoles in the creek, but Denzil was used to asphalt, and no one played with her. When a storm broke, lessons stopped and all the kids put on blue banana bags and pedalled home before the worst struck. When it rained Denzil had to wait by herself on the verandah until someone was driving her way.

There was a bike down in Sydney but there wasn't much point sending it up on the train because no one knew how long Denzil was staying on the farm. It might only be a couple more months, it might be forever, no one was really sure. It all depended on whether Auntie Gwen's back got better or whether Auntie Pat's daughter went nursing or whether Auntie Mim found Denzil too much or whether Uncle Clem really believed that blood was thicker than water. Whatever they decided, Denzil would have to do. When Denzil heard them talking about her she used to feel like something in the copper, swirling round and round and every so often lifted up by someone with a long smooth stick; she found herself wondering how long it would be before she would take on the same grey colour.

What Denzil herself wanted to do was run fast out of the valley and hide in the hills with Kylie. They'd live on bananas and rain and hunting. But now she couldn't dream that either, for one fine day Kylie went too far, and Uncle Clem wasn't a man for idle threats.

QUICKSAND

Sydney swelters in the doldrums of January as I trudge back from King Street with the shopping, pushing Melly in the stroller and saying 'No!' to the other two girls, who whine behind. No we can't go to the beach Kate, no we can't even go to the pool Jane, the car is at the garage ... 'I told you: no!'

As we turn the corner into Edward Street there is one of those sudden torrential summer storms, and we skelter down the hill beneath a cloud that cracks and splits its purple skin like a roasted eggplant. By the time we reach number 11, the steam rising from the pavement is the only sign left of the downpour. That, and the peppery smell of wet, dusty asphalt.

'Oh no!' gasps Kate, who is the drama merchant of the family. 'Oh no oh no oh no!'

For days I have been meaning to mend the lid on the letterbox, but it has been too hot for outdoor chores.

THE NIGHT TOLKIEN DIED

'Never mind,' I say, pulling out the mail, 'it'll only be envelopes with windows.'

Electricity. Bankcard (the Christmas presents still to be paid for, though already the kids are sick of them). The dentist. The Motor Registry. All bills. But there is also a very soggy postcard featuring a painting of a girl in a blue dress, standing on an empty stretch of sand with waves breaking on the rocks behind her. At the bottom right-hand corner of this picture of a girl in a blue dress there is superimposed a stamp-sized identical picture — indeed, I see now, a stamp — of the girl in the blue dress, for this postcard is apparently an Australia Post promotion for the release of this new stamp.

I remember the ice-cream melting and hurry inside to unpack, so it is a while before I actually sit down and turn the girl in the blue dress over, to see what message she has for me.

Oh no (as Katie would say). The handwriting is bold and hasty, and my correspondent has used thick black ink (I mean real fountain pen ink) that has splodged and run, so that I feel as if I am deciphering the Dead Sea Scrolls. Finally I manage to make out:

Hi!
Bet you're surprised to hear from me!

I look ahead to the end of the message, to see who 'me'

is, but it is quite hopeless. The signature is a flamboyant illegible scrawl that takes so much room that the writer has run right across the top of the address space. Lacking room for my name she (he?) has simply written *11 Edward St Newtown*. Never mind, keep going and the context will make it clear ...

> *To tell you the truth I hadn't thought of you in years, and then just now in the PO I happened to bump into*

I stare at the name. It has three letters, and the last is pretty certainly 'n'. The first has a long stroke with a loop at the front. The middle one must be a vowel. I turn the postcard this way and that. 'I happened to *bump into* ...' Jen? Jan? Or Jon? Or maybe even Ian? I must know half a dozen people called any one of those names. (Read on, MacDuff ...)

> *... to bump into _____ who gave me your address. The next minute, blow me down if I didn't see this pc of you in your blue dress in the stamp display case.*

I read the painting's accreditation: Brian Dunlop, *The Blue Dress*. I turn the postcard front side up again. Me?

Well, certainly I wasn't the model for this: I don't know any painters, and besides, I am fatter and have at least five grey hairs. But now that I stare at it, I guess I can see a certain similarity — not to me now, but to me of the past ...

No, that's not quite right either, because my nose is dreadfully snub, and the model's is aquiline, but suddenly I see what he (for some reason I feel sure now that it is a he) means, for it is the *blue dress* that is me.

That was mine.

Even when I was Melly's age, blue was always my favourite colour; I never went for pink. So that when finally it was time to buy a dress for the End of Year, End of School, Final Farewell Dance, I naturally chose a blue one. (This blue one. Or at least one this blue.)

I took Owen. Not a boyfriend, but the only boy who was my friend. And indeed, my only real friend.

I went to a girls' school, and I was in a comfortable enough gang of hockey players and prefects. I could get by. Yet none of the other girls was into the secret stuff I was into: like Shakespeare's sonnets, and modern verse drama, all the Metaphysicals, and the *Alexandria Quartet*. That's where Owen came in.

His parents and mine were part of the same church social club, meeting every couple of weeks for tennis or a barbecue or some fund-raising activity. As a couple of young atheists, Owen and I would escape from these gatherings and hide inside a cubby of oleander bushes, behind the tennis practice board, and lob lines of pentameter back and forth:

'Shall I compare thee to a summer's day?'

'Thou art more lovely and more temperate.'

'Rough winds do shake the darling buds of May.'

'And summer's lease hath all too short a date!'

Or if the Bard were having a bad day, we'd revel in 'Lilies that fester smell far worse than weeds'.

Once, I remember, we conducted an experiment: a pile of oxalis and paspalum and stuff versus a pile of white arum lilies that we stole from the Memorial Garden. We left them on top of the hall roof for a fortnight. A month. In fact, neither gave off a particularly noticeable pong. Ah, but the metaphorical lilies smelled of black treachery, we agreed.

If this all sounds overly intellectual, I should add that, like any kids, we talked about sex. Oh, not in the language of the schoolyard, but revelling in the far more evocative coarseness of the Metaphysicals. (I can remember us clutching each other with laughter at Donne's 'Flea', who sucks first the poet, then his girlfriend: 'Confesse it, this cannot be said/A sinne or shame, or losse of maidenhead' ...)

And of course we ourselves both wrote poetry. Though that was too secret to show, to speak about, even to each other.

So when the time came for the Orange Juice (as our school dance was dubbed because of its strictly teetotal nature) Owen was obviously the person I should ask to be my partner.

And yet ...

Owen was only in Year 11, and all the others were naturally asking Year 12 boys (except for Jennifer Whitlock, the school captain, whose boyfriend was at university!). And Owen was well over six foot, but he was skinny as a broomstick, and okay he didn't wear glasses, but his skin was like the craters of the moon. Besides — and I can see/say this now, although I couldn't understand it then; at the time it just felt like indescribable squeamishness — there seemed to be something *off* about asking Owen for a date. Like (I couldn't think this then) almost incest or something. For Owen was my mate, my soul, myself.

So I asked a girl called Marion to ask her boyfriend Tim to ask his friend Alan if he would go to the Orange Juice with me. (We'd met at a football match.) And Alan told Tim to tell Marion to tell me: yes.

Once that was settled, Mum and I went into town (to Mark Foys I remember; the shop doesn't exist any more) and I saw the blue dress and I knew: that's me.

And then a week before the dance, Alan rang up: he'd got his dates mixed, and next Saturday night was the Abbotsleigh Formal at the Chevron Hilton, and he'd already promised ...

I went round to Owen's place, and we discussed

Dostoevsky for an hour or two (I adored Raskolnikov, almost as much as I loved John Donne; Owen, being male, was somewhat less enthusiastic) and I eventually popped the question, and Owen of course agreed.

Of the night — of that night — I remember little. I can see us not dancing, but standing on the grass outside the assembly hall, sipping orange cordial from paper cups, talking about *Murder in the Cathedral*.

But perhaps I have made that bit up. And anyway it is irrelevant. For while the dance was the reason for the dress, it is not the explanation — of anything. And after all it is not as if the postcard could be from Owen, whom I haven't seen since —

'Cordial!' the girls yell now in my ear. 'You promised when we got home there'd be cordial.'

So I get it out, and make them drinks. If they do it themselves they leave sticky puddles and the ants come.

I realise as I wipe the bench that I've drifted into all this dress story before I've finished reading the postcard. Sitting down with it again, I finally make out:

> *... in the stamp display case.*
> *Talk about synchronicity!*
> *So felt I just had to get in touch. Happy*
> *New Year! (Remember N Y Eve 67?!)*
> *Best wishes,*
> *SquiggleSquoggle*

As the sound of television channel skirmishes (cricket versus cartoons; 'It was *your* turn this *morning!*' '*Mum!*') drift in from the next room, I go cold.

It is from Owen.

Oh no it can't be.

I mean I haven't seen him since —

New Year's Eve 1967. Or New Year's Day 1968. The catastrophe happened around midnight, but that is a movable feast at such moments — people start kissing early, and blowing hooters, letting off firecrackers, popping champagne corks, while other people go off for a piss, get back later, fail to adjust their clocks. Expect things to be the same, when they are not.

I know this: I didn't mean to.

I know this too: I'm not giving that as my excuse.

This is what happened:

That summer, Owen's parents rented a holiday unit down on the peninsula. There was always a big New Year's Eve dance at the yacht club — I'd heard about it, lots of girls from school went every year, but I'd never been.

Anyway, when Owen's family dropped in for the ritual exchange of presents after church on Christmas Day, Owen and I talked a bit — what options I'd take in Eng Lit — *if* I got into uni (I secretly knew that I would) — and what a drag it was that he had another year at school. (Owen was the same age as me, actually a couple of months older, but because his family had moved from interstate when he was in primary he'd ended up behind.) Finally he said, 'If you're not doing anything New Year's Eve, do you want to come down to Palm Beach and stay, and go to the yacht club dance?'

'Okay,' I said, pretending I didn't care, but swearing to go on a diet (can you lose half a stone in a week?), trying to think what to wear, imagining myself for the first time in my life really cracking the scene. Even if it was just going to be with Owen. (I knew we'd simply stand around and talk about T.S. Eliot, but that didn't matter: I liked talking about T.S. Eliot. But to talk about T.S. Eliot at the yacht club New Year's dance!)

So on the afternoon of the 31st I packed the blue dress, plus clean undies, new stockings, suspender belt (tights weren't invented in those days), my silver dancing shoes and my Oroton evening purse in a suitcase, and caught the bus down to Palm Beach.

Owen and his parents met me (Owen after a couple of days in the sun looking like a boiled lobster), we went back to the unit, I was given Owen's room (it was only a two-bedroom place, so Owen was going to have to sleep on the lounge), and I was told I had two hours to freshen up and have a rest and Get Ready.

I showered and went back to the room and I lay down

and tried to sleep and couldn't, and there was an exercise book next to the bed and honestly I didn't mean to do this, but of course I opened it — and of course it was full of bad teenage Eliot-style poetry.

That, in itself, wasn't what put me off.

But what was dreadful, appalling, and absolutely made me feel sick to the stomach was the fact that Owen's bad T.S. Eliot poetry was identical to everything I had been writing for the last couple of years. I saw myself as a sham (You? Old man Tiresias?!) and hated him for it. I would never write anything ever again.

I put on the blue dress and went to the dance.

There was a fat man at our table who insisted that Pimms was the drink for young ladies.

I was a young lady, so I had a few. The cucumber was so refreshing, you could rub it against your cheek after the dancing. And in the dancing, I managed to jig about a bit with Owen, despite the poetry. After all, I was his partner and the guest of his parents and I was a young lady (I drank Pimms, didn't I?) and the balcony was so refreshing after the dancing.

It was out there that I ran into Jennifer Whitlock. She was with her university boyfriend, who was with his mate Brook. Brook didn't go to university but he was quite the most fascinating conversationalist I had ever met. He didn't say a word that I could hear but he whispered in my ear as he danced with me. On the balcony.

Owen came out and I introduced them and I had an idea in my mind still that (despite the poetry) Owen was my friend but Owen went back inside for a piss and it wasn't my fault if the balcony was working on a faster clock than inside and people started blowing hooters, popping champagne corks, letting off rockets, kissing early, and Brook said 'Come down the beach ... ' and I said —

Nothing probably, but I went.

(Seeing Owen's face, lobster-red and simultaneously eggshell-white as I walked down the steps. Did I see that?)

Block out. Blank out. Do not remember. Listen to the children fighting in the next room. Think of the envelopes with windows. Anything.

Oh, it's not what happened on the beach with Brook that makes me blanch with shame. That was as normal — if as inept — as teenagers writing T.S. Eliot.

But to think that Owen would write me such a nice postcard, after what I did ...

New Year's Eve 1967/New Year's Day 1968:

I stayed out with Brook all night. After a time, down on the Pittwater side, below the yacht club, we went in his car (Brook had a car of course) to the surf beach.

We subsequently drank tinnies as dawn broke, but soon after that Brook had to go down the coast to catch a wave, and I walked up the beach (silver dancing shoes, stockings, suspenders, evening purse, all long gone, I noticed) sobering up and realising that I had no money and no way of getting home and I could not I could not I could not go back to Owen's parents' place. Even if I knew how to find it.

... It is now, looking at the postcard, that I see — not me, for thank Christ I had no mirror — but maybe me as Owen saw me that morning as he stood beside the dressing sheds with my suitcase, and I walked across the beach in my blue dress.

(Though surely I must have looked more shamed, more crestfallen? At least more terrified — because I knew that all hell would break out when — if? — I ever got home and my parents learned that I'd left Owen and his parents and the dance and disappeared and stayed out all night and ... ?)

All I saw, at the time, was that Owen too was still in his party clothes, and his sunburn was peeling off his face in slices. 'Here,' he said, handing me my things.

'But how ... '

At first he wouldn't speak, but finally he explained that as soon as I'd left, he had told his parents that there was a party, and we were going to it, and he'd left too.

He knew that his parents, my parents, would believe it was innocent if we were together. He had spent the night under the yacht club. Had crept home before his parents woke, and packed my gear. Then he'd come to find me ...

'Why?'

His look said everything. Why indeed? We were mates, we were each other (except now we weren't).

'Summer's lease ... ' I prompted, wanting him to rhyme with me. But I knew that everything was changed. (Oh sex, doing it, the losse of maidenhead, that wasn't the reason, for Owen and I were Metaphysicals; but the whiff of lilies out-stunk the sea kelp that day.)

I took the suitcase and went into the Ladies and changed into the clothes I'd worn down on the bus. Rolled the blue dress into a ball and stuffed it into the cistern. When I came out, Owen was gone.

I never saw him again. (Unable to face him, I pleaded pressure of uni essays to avoid the barbecues and get togethers of the next twelve months, and the following January I heard that he had gone to Armidale Uni to study Agriculture, of all things. Then my parents retired, moved to the north coast, and soon it was as if Owen and his family had disappeared from the face of the earth.)

Now, feeling the warmth of his friendship, the

absolution of the postcard, I read, scrawled around on the side: *Am in town for a few days so might drop in to see you, now that I know where to find you,* and I pray: Oh yes, please do, I'd so love to see you.

But suddenly think: what if this is Brook?

I mean the facts (no, fact — one fact — *Remember N Y Eve 67?!*) would fit just the same.

What if Brook ____ (it is pointless to try to read the signature because I never knew his surname) ran into Ian/Jon/Jan/Jen (Jennifer Whitlock? I saw her last year at the class reunion; maybe swapped addresses) at the PO and started gossiping about (I shudder to think) and my name came up and he saw the postcard and he ...

And what if Brook, now knowing where to find me, drops in?

I read the postcard again. *'Synchronicity'*. The conjunction of things through a coincidence of time. Brook would never use a word like that. It must be Owen. But *'blow me down'* didn't sound like Owen. (Did it sound like Brook? I couldn't say. He just danced into my empty ear.)

But staring again now at the signature, at the mess the rain has made of the ink, it suddenly seems to me that it is possibly not 11 Edward Street at all, but 111 that the postcard is addressed to.

'Where are you going, Mum?'

'Back in a minute! Look after Mel!'

I run up the hill through the heat, hoping, not hoping...

But 111 is a factory site: no girl in a blue dress lives there.

So I return and put the dinner on, pour myself a beer, and it is as I find myself ridiculously waiting for a knock at the door that I get out the postcode book:

Newtown NSW

Newtown Vic

Newtown (Ipswich) Qld

Newtown (Toowoomba) Qld

And then there is New Town Tas and Newton SA.

There's no postcode on the card. And there must be Edward Streets everywhere. Leaving aside the issue of whether it is 11 or 111.

Treading carefully now through the quicksand of memory that I have stirred up for myself, I look again at the picture with its superimposed stamp, and I see girls in blue dresses multiplying unto soft eternity on endless strands of empty beaches.

And now that I think of it, SquiggleSquoggle's handwriting is so bad that 67 could as well be 61. Which would conjure up a totally different series of stories again ...

I am grinning with relief as my three girls come out.

'Hey Mum, whatcha doin?'

'Oh no, you're not still reading that silly old thing?'

'Whatsit say?'

'What do you reckon, Mel?' I reply.

Melly takes the postcard and with the fluency of a three year old reads the picture in a flash: 'There's this lady at the seaside ... '

'Hey Mum, c'n we go to the beach tomorrow?' Kate says.

'I told you, no!'

'In a yaller dress ... '

'Not yaller,' I start, 'yellow. And anyway it's ... '

'She's lost her dog,' Mel goes on, 'so she's calling *Here puppy here puppy here!*'

'Hey Mum,' says Kate, 'hey Mum, c'n we get a dog?'

'Of course we can,' I gush, 'my darling girl!' (As if by going to the pound and rescuing a stray I can somehow make the picture take on Melly's meaning.)

I plant a kiss on Kate's amazed face as Jane interrupts, 'But what does it really say, Mum?'

'I think,' I say, 'it is saying *Don't look back* ... ' Knowing now that even if it *were* Owen, it would be too late: for a mother of three with greying hair and a mass of bills cannot, even through the magic of synchronicity, change back into a carefree girl playing poetry in an oleander cubby.

'By the way,' Kate says, 'when you were out, a man came and knocked at the door.'

'We didn't answer it,' Jane adds virtuously.

LISTENING TO MONDRIAN

Call me Jo.

That's not my name. But it sure makes our father wild.

Jonathon. That's what he calls me. *'Meet my son Jonathon.'* Never Jon or Jonnie or Jonno. Even when I was a really little kid it was always the full bit, and of course never any of those affectionate nicknames (Sonny-Jim, Kiddo, Buster, Bugalugs) that fathers call their sons.

Maybe that's why I've always had lots of different names for people. Like Gemma is Gem and Gemstone and Gemfish and Fishface and even Little Fishter and of course Sis and Bub and Bud and sometimes really weird things like Murgatroyd and Captain Starlight and Mr Palfreyman.

And *he* is Dad when I address him in public (said in the deep manly voice that he likes) and Daddy when

Gem speaks to him (said in the high girly voice that he likes). But he is the Pater (isn't that word great? I found it in a snobby English school story) when he comes to get me from school and has a pompous little chat with the Reverend Dr Principal about 'the lad's future'. And he is Papa when he is strolling along the boulevardes with a Maurice Chevalier air. And he is Father when he presides at the dining table. And he is also Hitler, Stalin, Mussolini, Ghenghis Khan, and Phalaris the tyrant of Agracas. (That's the guy who used to put his victims inside the bronze cast of a bull and then roast them alive over a slow fire. The gory bits of Ancient History are my best subject.)

As for my mother, poor bloody sod, once upon a time she was Mummy, but he thought it was sissy for me to call her that so then she was Mum. She was never Mother (that was part of the problem) and neither was she Mademoiselle of the Boulevardes (though he had plenty of substitutes; that was part of the problem too). She was the Boss's Wife for a while, when he brought visiting execs home for dinner, but she was too shy for that, just a simple country girl and a plain cook as well, and so she became Old Mother Macreadie, with her hair in a scarf and gin bottle at hand. And then eventually (and still) she was Mad Mrs Rochester (you know, the loony wife in *Jane Eyre* who is kept locked up and secret in the west wing or wherever; in Mum's case it's an expensive clinic in Switzerland, but it amounts to the same thing).

And me — well I am Jon to the younger teachers, Frazier to the older ones, and to my mates I am Fraz or Frazzles or Speedy Gonzales (I'm one of the wingers in the First XV), and for one brief week after I scored the winning try in the Greater Public Schools Grand Final I was Campo (as in David Campese). To my enemies, on the other hand, I guess I'm all sorts of names, though I haven't got to hear them since the day when I was in Year 9 and one of the prefects said something about alkie mothers and I decked him so radically that he was in the sick bay for a week.

But the nicest thing I am is Jo. That's what Gemfish calls me. In the Good Old Days Mum used to read to her at night, and one of the things was this poem that goes:

Jonathon Jo
Has a mouth like an 'O'
And a wheelbarrow full of surprises ...

Sis picked up on it, I think partly because she had trouble with her 'th' sounds, and if she said 'Jonafon' Father would make her sit at the dinner table or even in the bath saying '*Th-th-th-th thing, thong, Jonathon!*' Poor kid got so demented about it that she would take a deep breath and make an explosive *'th'* sound on all the wrong words too. So she said *'that'* as the opposite to *'thin'* and on *'Thridays* we had *'thish* and chips' and one day she told me to *'Thuck oth!'* All in all, Jo was easier.

But besides that, I guess when she was a little kid (she's only nine now, so I mean when she was really little) and we lived together, I guess I maybe did seem full of surprises to her. Like the day when I said 'Open your mouth' and she did and I squirted the soda water siphon down her gullet. Or the day when I told her that if you eat a handful of little red birdseye chillies you go invisible. To be fair to me though, there were sometimes nice surprises too, such as doubling her on my bike to the beach and teaching her to be safe in the water. ('Just to the first line of little breakers, and always keep your eyes on the flags, Gem!') Or making a fort for her to hide in or showing her how to burn dead paspalum stalks with a magnifying glass. Or holding her when Mum was taken away.

These days, of course, I don't see Bub much. We board at different schools, and in the holidays she goes to old Auntie Roo's and I'm sent to Tennis Camp and Maths Camp and Computer Camp et cetera. So we only get to meet on days like today, when the Great White Chief jets in from OS, arrives unexpectedly at our schools and takes us out of class and off to the museum or the gallery, then (always) the Royal Sydney Golf Club Dining Room for lunch, a stroll (he calls it 'a postprandial constitutional') around Centennial Park, and back to the lock-up in time for him to jet out again on the peak hour super-shuttle to Wall Street or wherever.

Last time (five months ago) it was the museum, so today it's the gallery.

'I thought I'd take them to see the Guggenheim,' the Pater told the Rev Dr Prickhead this morning when I was pulled out of first period maths. (Hurray for that at least!)

'The Guggenheim?' I said. 'What's that when it's at home?' Joke. I mean, I do know that the Guggenheim is a gallery in the Big Apple, and that they've got the pest exterminators in or something at the moment, so they've sent a collection out to Sydney so us yokel Down-underers can get to see a real live Picasso at first hand. So I do know that the Guggenheim's home is in New York City, and it's not at home now, and — oh, forget it.

'... Lack of general knowledge,' complained the person who paid the school fees.

The Rev Dr Browntongue squirmed. 'But I believe his mathematics is picking up. What was it you got in the yearly exams, boy?'

'Nineteen.'

LISTENING TO MONDRIAN

'*Out of a hundred?*' An explosion was starting, but good old Gemfish (Dad had picked her up first) put on one of her cute-as-a-button acts.

'Oh come on, Daddy, you said you were taking me to see the pretty pictures, you promised...'

Don't overdo it, Shirley Temple, I thought, but it actually worked. (Owe you one, Gem!)

So here we are.

Standing at the cash register while our father has an argument about my age (I'm just seventeen but can pass for eighteen in any pub, and I got away with twenty-one at half-term, when a mate and I wanted to suss out a dirty bookshop).

'He is only fifteen,' Dad argues, though whether because he's forgotten or because he's scared the child concession limit might be sixteen, I don't know. (The thing I should explain here is that our father is mean as catshit. Oh, in order to get rid of us he'll pay for expensive boarding schools and tennis camps and crap, but when we go out for lunch we're allowed the main course and *either* an entree *or* a dessert but never both. And I have seen him bend down and pick up a one cent coin that someone has dropped on the footpath. Truly. Despite the fact that he is some sort of big wheel money-mover who zots trillions around the international Monopoly Board via his fax machine.)

'Can't you see he's in school uniform, woman?' he demands.

The cash register lady peers at me. I'm in my school suit of course, but the badge on the breast pocket is pretty faded and the tie could be any boring Old School Tie. Meanwhile the queue behind us has stacked back to the dunnies and beyond.

'Oh very well! One adult, two kiddies!' She zings the amount up on the till. 'Twenty-six dollars.'

But our father isn't finished. This is an Educational Experience, you understand, not bloody Bush Week, so we are all to have these personal cassette recorders you can hire for three dollars with a tape inside that tells you how to look at the pictures.

We get our recorders, and the lady adds nine dollars to the bill, but now Dad realises that it's possible to double up two ear plugs to the one recorder and save a whole dollar. So Murgatroyd gets her recorder taken off her, and she is made to plug into my recorder, and the bill is finally agreed upon and our father flips his gold American Express card out of his wallet in his inside breast pocket (the queue groans) and he signs with a flourish and finally we are off: Dad way out in front like the Lord of the Manor, and Sis and me attached through the recorder like a couple of Siamese twins.

Me and my shadow ...' I start softly singing to her as

the cassette plays a short burst of trumpet music. (`Welcome,' says a voice, 'to Cubism, Abstraction, Surrealism and Expressionism ...')

'Shut *up,*' Bub complains. 'It's not *funny!*'

And I have to agree that while it isn't funny for me to be trailing along in public with a plump little nine year old with pigtails and thick specs and her school socks fallen down round her ankles, it's even less funny for her because her legs are half the length of mine and she has to do two steps and a skip to my one stride.

'Slow *down,* Jo!'

So I do, and that's how we lose him by the end of STOP NUMBER 1: Pablo Picasso, *Carafe, Jug and Fruit Bowl 1909.*

I look up, and the Captain has left the sinking ship.

'... When you are ready, go through the archway,' the tape tells us, and explains that there is a little jingle in between each STOP, and when you hear that you have to turn the tape off and proceed to the next numbered picture stop. It's all a bit like musical chairs, or pass the parcel.

We don't have to look at anything in Room 2, which is good because I can already see (just around the corner in Room 3) something that is blowing my mind. It turns out to be STOP NUMBER 2: four pictures by some painter called Robert Delaunay.

THE NIGHT TOLKIEN DIED

This guy's really cool.

First there's one of spooky arches all sort of receding from each other, like a trick mirror that lets you see yourself going on for ever and ever and ever. You could lose yourself down that corridor of arches, no risk. (Maybe that's where our Fearless Leader has got to. Very funny, Jo.)

Then there's a skewiff picture of *The City 1911*. Next there's something called *Eiffel Tower 1911*. Of course, I've seen the Eiffel Tower on TV — who hasn't? — but this is better than television, or even real life. Somehow the building is kind of tilted so it seems to be floating above the city, among all these white and yellow clouds, and the other buildings round it sort of bend, like saplings in a wind. And next to that there's a painting of a smaller, *red* Eiffel Tower (the first one was pink).

In all these pictures, it looks as if the buildings are sort of collapsing into each other. That makes it sound as if there's been a bomb or something but it's not violent like that. It's as if the turning of the earth is something that you can really feel, shifting you around in the gentlest of circles. And it's like ... you know when you're about to go to sleep — you're almost dreaming — then suddenly you feel yourself drop about 200 metres through sheer space? And it's scary, but also exciting, and somehow a bit sexy too at the same time?

That's what Delaunay's city was like.

But speaking of dreams, I guess talking about pictures is about as thrilling as when some guy at breakfast reckons 'You'd never guess what I dreamed last night!' And you all go, 'Oh no, you weren't stuck in a lift with Madonna again were you? Pass the cornflakes someone please ...'

So suffice it to say (as the Rev Dr says: 'Suffice it to say that the name of the boy who was smoking in the box room at 7.27 pm on Sunday is not unknown to me ...') suffice it to say that we listen to:

STOP NUMBER 3: *Statue of Adam and Eve* by Brancusi. (Gem giggles: it's like huge wooden bosoms and balls sitting on top of a giant corkscrew.)

STOP NUMBER 4: Marc Chagall, *Paris Through the Window 1913*. (Gem likes this: there's an upside-down train and a cat with a lady's face.)

STOP NUMBER 5: *Nude 1917* and *Jeanne Hebuterne with Yellow Sweater* by Amedeo Modigliani.

To get here, we've gone through into another room, that leads in turn to a couple more big rooms. We are just finishing Modigliani and the tape guy is telling us that at STOP NUMBER 6 we'll see the paintings of Piet Mondrian, when through the next archway I spot Papa.

Oh yes, make no mistake, it is Papa now. From the other side of the gallery you can almost smell the characteristic combination of French champagne and candlelight and gypsy violins and twelve-red-roses-by-special-delivery and (yes, I'm afraid) dirty old tomcat too.

He is ooooooooozing.

She is — (words fail me).

Well, for a start, she is tall, very slender (on someone else it'd look anorexic), blonde streaked hair in a French plait, age (??) twenty-two last birthday at the most. Wearing a creamy-coloured sleeveless little tunic-thing that would look like a flour sack on anyone else but on her ...

Bare legs. Bare brown l-o-n-g legs that are smooth as silk. They end in feet that somehow turn you on, the way they're trapped in these open-toe lizard skin sandals with high high heels that seem to make her bottom noticeable. (To put it mildly.)

Around her throat is a single strand of pearls.

'Get a look at this!' I nudge, but my shadow twin is absorbed in Art.

When Gemmy was a little kid, before we knew she had bad eyes, she used to get right up close to things (the television; the cat; my face) and sort of seem to get entranced by what she saw, she studied it so hard. I guess that's maybe why I liked her so much: it's very flattering, when you're ten years old and someone (even your two-year-old sister) comes up and gazes and gazes at you, as if you're Superperson or something.

I guess she was four or five when Mum worked out that there was maybe some reason for this close staring (that was towards the end of the Good Old Days, but still at a time when Mum was able to work things out and Dad was home often enough for her to tell him) and so Gem was taken to the doc and got her glasses.

The doc said she was short-sighted, but very astigmatic too. 'Asthmatic,' I thought Mum said when she told me but Mum said no, ast-*ig*-matic isn't wheezing and gasping. Ast*i*gmatic is when the rays of light sort of converge unequally in the lens of the eye, so everything seems to have odd angles and sometimes things look as if they're somewhere else from where they really are. (e.g. Sis pouring milk was always the drama of the breakfast table when Father was home. She'd miss by a mile, and be yelled at or — worse — demolished with sarcasm. And of course when it finally turned out it was because the glass for her was in a different place to where it really was, Father just said Mum should have noticed sooner. What sort of mother was she? etc, etc.)

Anyway, what I'm trying to say is that a couple of years ago, Little Fishter went back to her staring act. When she does it, she seems to go way off with the fairies somewhere — you could stick a pin in her and she wouldn't blink, let alone scream.

That's what she does now, when I try to draw her attention to the Dynamic Duo. (He must be getting all hot and bothered: he's taken his coat off, I see.)

Nudge nudge. 'Hey Weezlebumps, get a dekko at this!'

But Papa and Helen of Troy could be rooting on the floor for all the difference it would make to my learned friend the eminent art critic.

She is right up close to *Composition 1938-39* by Pete (his real name's Piet but I call him Pete for short) Mondrian. Here the tape guy goes on about something called Concrete Painting (which sounds like it ought to be done on concrete but it's just done on canvas like all the others). And he reckons there's a lot of maths in Mondrian too, which I'd agree with, because the pictures are basically rectangles done in the sort of colours that kindergarten kids use.

'The paintings of Franz Marc are our next STOP — that's NUMBER 7,' the tape reckons now, but it doesn't look as if we'll ever make it because my better half sits, yes sits down plop on the floor, crosses her legs, places her hands in her lap, and continues to gaze (upwards now) at *Composition 1938-39.*

Of course, when she sits, there's a jerk on the cassette recorder, and I feel like a dog pulled up short on a lead. I guess I could disconnect her plug and leave her here by herself.

However, you don't just leave little girls totally unsupervised in strange places and besides, I'm a bit weary on the whole thing myself by now, so after a little while I sit down beside her. (*'Yeah man, like this is a sit-in, OK?'* Who knows, maybe if we make a public spectacle of ourselves Dad'll get so embarrassed he'll come and take us out to lunch. Personally speaking, I could eat a horse right at this minute, and chase the rider.)

But if Gemstone can go blind at will, so can (maybe it's hereditary?) our father.

We sit and sit, and the tape runs on, though I turn it down now till it's just a drone — white noise I think it's called, when electronic signals are transmitted in a way to have a sort of sound-masking effect ...

And come to think of it, *White Noise* would be a good name for this picture, not that it really is a *picture,* just ...

I'll give you the recipe:

Take a piece of white canvas, about one metre square.

With black paint, do three lines down the right-hand side and one down the left-hand side, like prison bars. Then do four black lines horizontally from the left-hand side of the canvas to the first of the vertical right-hand lines. Then, in the middle and at the very bottom, do another black line across the canvas, right through the prison window.

Now, with red paint fill in a little rectangle (about 3 cm x 10 cm) that has been made at the bottom of the picture by the meeting of the horizontal and vertical black lines.

That's it.

It's not a lot to look at but I sit and I sit ...

Suddenly I do my block. Oh, I don't jump up, rant and rave, yell and scream, storm over to our father and demand: 'Who the fuck do you think you are, treating us like this? How dare you pretend to take us out for the day and then leave us, dump us, let us sit for hours in front of the stupidest picture in the universe while you chat up some new floozy!'

I don't do that, not outwardly, but inwardly I do. I say everything imaginable and unimaginable. I remind him how, last time, back in July, Gem ended the day in tears because Daddy kept telling his little Sugarplum that she was too fat and he wouldn't let her have her favourite — strawberries — for dessert, even though she'd forgone the entree. (Oysters are her other favourite.)

I remind him how, the time before that, back in January, he arrived with our (late as always) Christmas presents: a mathematics computer program for me and a globe of the world for Sis. Wow. The cream of it was that he'd given Sis a globe of the world the Christmas before, too.

Now it gets really bad and I start reminding him how he drove Mum to where she is. Oh yes. When he met her she was (I think I said) a simple country girl, who thought a drink meant a shandy at New Year for the sake of auld lang syne. But when Golden Boy got his first big promotion he decided that he liked her to be all dressed up and waiting when he got home, with a martini in the shaker and olives in the glass. So she started doing that, but he started coming home later and later, or not at all, and the ice started to melt and the martini was going warm so there was no solution but to drink it, was there? I mean, he doesn't like *waste*.

Soon it was straight gin, pass on the vermouth, forget about the olives too.

It only took a couple of years — from when I was in Year 7 to when I was in Year 9 — for Old Mother Macreadie to get right into it. I'd come home from footy training and Gem would be glued to the TV screen and Ma would already have passed out for the night. I'd dial a pizza, pay for it out of Mum's purse, feed the kid, put her to bed, watch the box, go to bed myself, and wait for the sound of the Porsche down the drive.

Then all hell would break loose.

She'd have slept enough of the gin off by then for him to wake her with his abuse: *slag, slut, slackarse;* he called her every name in the book — and all the names that don't get into books, too. And it was quite untrue. I mean, she may have been a drunk, but as far as sex was concerned, *he* was the one who was playing around.

One night, she wasn't there but — was she?

I must've dozed off, not heard her slip out.

They found her the next morning on the railway track.

Oh, she was okay, dead to the world but not real deadybones dead. Silly sausage, she'd been so pissed she'd gone and lain down on a disused goods line.

That was the end.

Off she whizzed on an aeroplane to this clinic (read loony bin) in snowy Switzerland. We weren't even allowed to say goodbye at the airport. Gemma howled and I held her, but then we were taken away from each other. Once we were safely at boarding school, Adolf could whizz off too. Next time I saw the little Gemfish, I realised she'd relearnt the stare-and-disappear trick. (Maybe red hot birdseye chillies do work after all. I mean, Sis can make the whole *world* invisible!)

So I'm raging, okay? Raging right back through the record (I told you the gory bits of Ancient History are my best subject) as I watch our father do his suavo-sleaso act upon this new chick.

Red/red/red/red/red/red/red/red — I find myself focusing all my anger through the bit at the bottom of the picture, as I stare through the prison bars.

And then suddenly now I slip.

I can't say it any other way.

It's a bit like that dream-falling, but less dramatic, not a plunge, just a kind of amoeba-jelly slide through the black lines and into the white space that opens before me like the avenue of Delaunay's archways, only even more infinite.

Maybe it's because we're like two divers connected to the same air tank, but somehow as I sit joined to my sister listening to the white noise of Mondrian through the cassette deck I find myself moving into the space that she finds when she disappears.

I can't say any more, because it is not a place of words or even feelings, it is just —

I do not know how long we sit but the refuge is such that when our father appears beside us I feel free of him. He cannot hurt me any more. Or not today. I am beyond the bars, and far away.

'This is Miss Silkin. Would you believe it, she works here in our Sydney branch, we met last year, and then just happened to bump into each other ...'

No, I would not believe it. But do not give a shit either. (Look, here's the other leg: why don't you pull that too?)

'... Unfortunately however, Miss Silkin happened to mention a little problem that has just cropped up on the Tokyo exchange ...'

(What, does she carry a fax machine in that lizard skin handbag?)

'... And so I'm afraid that I'll have to take a raincheck on our lunch, and pop into our office here ...'

It's so transparent, I could laugh. But just say that's okay, I'll get a cab, drop Gemmy back at her school, then go on to mine.

'Oh, by the way,' he turns to his colleague, 'meet my son Jonathon. And this is my daughter Gemma. Miss Silkin.'

'Oh call me Louisa,' she protests.

'Hi, Lulu!' I grin, but Dad is hurrying us off too fast to even notice.

Back to the cash register. The queue now has all the lunchtime art lovers but Stalin isn't in a mood for stalling. 'We're just returning these.' He barges through the front of the line and yanks — truly yanks — the earplugs from Gem's and my ears, hoists the airtank off me, and stacks the lot on the desk.

'Here, hold this.' He dumps his suit coat into my arms.

'Be with you in a moment, Louisa ...' And disappears into the toilet. Ah, so that's the cause of all the urgency.

Louisa murmurs something to Gemma and they disappear too.

The idea comes as a flash: here's your chance, Jo. And I take it.

Coming out into sunshine I feel free as a bird let out of its cage.

Dad hands me a twenty dollar note to cover the taxi fare, changes his mind, makes it a ten and a five, and I feel even better. Mingy bastard.

A cab pulls up, and now Dad's last concern is over. 'Well, Jonathon. Well, Gemma.' He opens the car door and almost pushes us in. 'I won't be back again before Christmas but I will bring your presents some time in the new year ...'

(After all, we wouldn't want to waste money on postage, would we? It doesn't worry me, but I know Murgatroyd is always disappointed if she doesn't get something on The Day.)

'Bye, Dad.'

'Bye bye, Daddy.'

But he is off. And so are we.

'Just drop us at the quay, please,' I tell the driver.

Gemma's eyes sparkle. She is well and truly back now from the place she disappears to far inside. 'Where're we going, Jo?'

'Lunch,' I tell her.

'But where?'

'You'll see.'

'Oh Jo ... go on ...'

We pull up now and the little Fishface eyes are goggling through their aquarium glass as they take in where we are. 'Oh Jo! We're not! We're not truly, are we? Are we?'

'Are we what?' I tease.

'Going to the — you know — the Revolting Restaurant!' she explodes with joy.

It's really revolving, of course, and she knows it, but once upon a time in the Good Old Days when Ghenghis Khan was still just your common or garden family fascist and not the High Panjandrum of Them All, we went on an outing — Dad, Mum, and the two kids — to this restaurant that revolves around in a circle as you eat. Little Gem-baby (she would've been about four at the time) called it revolting instead of revolving, and we all laughed (our family *laughed*, I can distinctly remember it) and so she said it again and we laughed again, and she said it again and we ... Well, to tell you the truth Daddy got sick of it by the third go and made his Baby Bunting cry, but it was good while it lasted, and ever since then Sis has always begged please couldn't we go to the Revolting Restaurant instead of the Royal Sydney Golf Club Dining Room? Daddy? Just once?

I tell you, just this once I hope and pray that Daddy takes his guest to the Royal Sydney, and not to some little restaurant that Lulu happens to know. At the Royal Sydney, see, he's a member, so he just tabs it up on his account.

Of course he will, I reassure myself. He's as reliable as Mussolini's train timetable. Then with any luck it'll be off to her place (she'd have to live in the Eastern Suburbs, no risk) for a bit of nookie, and finished in time to catch a taxi (he uses Cabcharge vouchers, so that's okay) to Mascot for the commuter special to New York.

All in all, I congratulate myself as the lift arrives at the zillionth floor and we exit into the restaurant foyer ...

I sort of drape my arm across my pocket badge, pull myself up to my full height.

'Monsieur? Mademoiselle?'

'A table for two,' I tell the waiter. 'By the window if possible. Mademoiselle likes to enjoy the view.'

'But of course, Monsieur.'

The place is three-quarters empty. They'd be mad to quibble at a couple of customers, even if the monsieur does look a bit deformed with his arm across his chest and the mlle is dancing for joy through the empty tables.

We are seated. Are given the menus. The wine list, sir? No worries. I take my coat off.

All in all, I congratulate myself again as I scan the wine list (French champagne? Why not? It's a special occasion after all. Only a half bottle, though. Don't want to get like Ma), with any luck he'll be in New York tomorrow morning (or last night or whatever time it'll be in NY when he arrives) before he realises what he's lost.

'Jo, *how?*' Sis is nearly exploding with curiosity. 'Did Daddy give you some money to spend?'

'He certainly did.'

I go like James Bond or something and open my coat, which hangs from my chair, and let her see the flash of dull gold which I transferred from his inside pocket into mine.

'Oh Jo Jo! Don't you feel guilty?'

'Gemmles, it's not *stealing,*' I explain carefully to her. (I don't want the kid to get the idea that you can just go and take people's things.) 'It's like when we were with Mum, remember? And she wasn't able to feed us, and I used to take money from her purse and buy us a pizza. Dad wasn't able to feed us today, and if we went back to school now, we'd have missed boarders' lunch. So I just helped him do his duty. It's the *law*, Bub. Fathers *have* to feed their children.'

LISTENING TO MONDRIAN

Gemma isn't as dumb as some people think. Once she gets the hang of the situation, she reads the menu with enthusiasm.

'Do we just have to have an entree and a main course, or a main course and a dessert, or can we have ...?'

'Anything you like, Princess,' I tell her.

In the end, she decides to skip the middle, and settles for a dozen oysters kilpatrick followed by strawberry chantilly with cream and ice-cream, and a glass of Coke.

'Just half a dozen oysters natural for me,' I tell the waiter, 'and for my main course, the grilled gemfish ...' I tease.

Sis splutters. 'Cannibal!'

'Make that the lobster thermidor, with a double serve of garlic bread, chocolate mudcake for dessert, and a half bottle of ...' I change my mind again, remembering how boring it is for little kids when people drink, 'I mean a large bottle of Coke. In an ice bucket, if we may.'

'Of course, Monsieur.'

I could really take to this sort of thing, I think, as the city down below us slowly shifts and shifts again, like the gentle collapse of a Delaunay. But one thought leads to another, and after a while I think of a worry.

'You know when you go away, Sis ...'

'In the holidays? To Auntie Roo's?'

'No — *away*. Like you did inside the picture ...'

She gives me a guilty look. Dad always yells at her for dreaming.

'It's okay,' I start to reassure her.

'You did too!' she accuses.

I sure did. As she says it, the feeling comes back, of the space inside there. I don't know of course if I'll ever get there again. And actually, I'm not sure that I want to. But this one time, listening to Mondrian has been enough to let me go beyond the prison bars. And if you've escaped once, I reckon, you probably become like Zorro or the Scarlet Pimpernel or something: you're always able to break free, one way or another.

But there's still this worry ...

'You don't go too far, do you?' That's all I want to know. I have a nightmare suddenly of me searching through the archways, trying to find my little gemfish as she flicks away into the wide white yonder ...

'Oh no,' she tells me earnestly. 'I used to nearly, when I was little, and then after Mum went away, I was going to go for good. But I didn't want to miss you. And then, I dunno. I learnt to do it like swimming, just to the first line of breakers and keep watching the flags on the shore, like you showed me. I don't do it much, you know. Just in class sometimes, when the arithmetic goes all jangly on the board. And when Daddy's — you know.'

'I know.'

We toast each other:

'Here's to us.'

'Here's to us, too.'

'Here's to us two, too.'

When the bill comes, I go like the ads: 'You take American Express?'

'But of course, Monsieur.'

I sign the signature with a flourish. Add in a generous sum for a tip.

'Thank *you*, Monsieur.'

'Any time,' I lie.

'What now?' Sis urges as we hit the streets. 'What about the zoo? Or the aquarium? Or ...'

I explain that we have no cash. 'A liquidity problem, you might say ...'

Bubba's face falls. 'So it's back to school.'

'Well ... as long as we stick to places where they take plastic, we could go Christmas shopping first ...'

Gem lights up again. 'After all, he *owes* us prezzies. That's the law.'

'I could get you a globe of the world,' I suggest.

'And I could get you a wheelbarrow.'

'A wheelbarrow?'

'*You* know,' my Gemini-twin prompts, 'to fill with surprises ...'

WOMEN'S BUSINESS

I realise now that she must have been in her late twenties when I loved her. I was nine.

('How old *are* you?')

('Old enough to know better.')

('Oh go on, tell me ...')

(Through the long hot afternoons.)

All I knew then was that she was a grown-up; but I also knew that it wasn't just age that made you one. The girl on the next farm down from ours was twenty-six and had a fiancé but was just a girl. Whereas anyone could see that *she* was grown-up because she was married and had money and her own little house and did whatever she wanted. One summer I stayed in town with her to get away from all the boys at our place. I used to wish that I could be solitary and free like a married woman, like her.

It was lovely, what she used to do.

She would lie in bed dozing and listening to the radio till about ten in the morning, and then get up and eat Saos with sardines or baked beans (or sometimes both) straight out of the tin for breakfast. Then she'd go back to bed and read women's magazines and smoke cigarettes. If she didn't feel like getting dressed, she wouldn't. She was extremely fat and always said that clothes made her hot. They made me hot too, and when I stayed with her I lived in my swimming costume. At my house I always had to be fully dressed by the time Mum served up the porridge, and I had to stay that way till after tea. *She* used to wear her faded pink nighties around the house and out in the yard; if she was going up to the corner shop to buy a loaf of bread, she'd just slip on a brunch coat.

The bread was another thing: we always had sliced at home 'because it goes further with all you kids', and Mum's sandwiches were so thin that the jam crept right through them and out into your suitcase. But the loaves that *she* bought had a high crusty top and was divided into two round humps. When you pulled the halves apart you had two doughy ends, one rising into a soft mountain, the other making a cavern that just held your clenched fist. The shop doorway was hung with one of those curtains made of long coloured plastic streamers to stop the flies, and she'd already be breaking open the bread as we fought our way back out like intrepid explorers. Sometimes the hard bright strips would catch around her neck, or whip across her breasts, around her waist. More and more would loop in then as she fought, and she'd laugh like anything while sweat started to trickle down her face and she'd call back at the shop people as she cleared the way with her fat little hands:

'Don't nobody help me!'

The black strips were the snakes and all the rest were the creeping jungle. I'd be jumping from bare foot to bare foot on the hot asphalt path, keeping a lookout for enemies. Once she was safe she'd give me the cave half and keep the mountain half herself, and we'd dig tunnels as we traipsed the hundred yards or so home.

Once we got there, we'd eat more bread with jam and butter *and* cream (though my home was a dairy farm, my family only had cream for lunch on Saturdays), or with tomato and onion and sugar and vinegar, or with lashings of golden syrup. And then tinned pears and ice cream. At her place there was dessert for lunch as well as for tea.

We'd be sitting by the fan on the small back verandah, listening to the news and 'Blue Hills'. She'd be drinking Passiona from a Jetty Hotel schooner glass and

WOMEN'S BUSINESS

I'd have Creaming Soda from the bottle.

'Must get the house straight,' she'd sigh next, but we'd stay there watching the dead grass and dust pools in the backyard, the lantana next to the dunny, the paspalum in the empty lot next door. I'd jig around a bit, wishing there wasn't a drought so I could turn on the sprinkler and run under, and she would move slowly around on her chair, rearranging the flesh inside the pink nightie, mopping at the trickle of sweat between her huge breasts, saying occasionally, 'Jeez love, it's hot,' lighting Craven As, stubbing them out in her dessert plate.

After that she'd go back to bed, taking the fan, the radio, the cigarettes, forgetting the ashtray. The house seemed to abound in ashtrays — including the kind I liked, with a sort of knob on a spring that you pressed down to send all the butts into the bowl — but she mostly used makeshift ones. Apart from plates and cups and saucers she would use shells and matchboxes and soft drink bottles of course, but also Nescafe tins, jam lids, bottle tops, teaspoons, cotton reels (she pushed the butts down into the hole), vases, lipstick cases, little round pots that still held lingers of cold cream or rouge. Though I objected to the smell when my mother had one of her social-occasional cigarettes, these doodahs of hers never even made me screw my nose up. Her messiness was simply proof of her freedom.

Yet another sign of her supreme independence was the bulging red purse which she carried in her fat three-ringed left hand whenever we went up the street. In her right she carried the cigarettes in a cracked gold kid case, and this was deputed to me whenever the right hand was needed to hold the bread, or a double vanilla cone. (I don't remember her ever buying anything apart from bread or cigarettes or ice cream or lollies; nor do I remember ever wondering where the pears and Spam and Pecks Paste came from, or the Sweet Mustard Sauce or Iced Vovos or pineapple rings, or the tins of beetroot that she would devour, juice and all.) When the girl who lived on the next farm down from ours took me into town for shopping, she'd have her mother's red purse, and she couldn't buy me green frogs and pink-and-white false teeth because it was 'Mum's money'. Moreover, she had to go to work every day (she was the secretary at the Co-op) and never stayed in bed. Even on Saturdays she had to wash her hair and iron her work clothes and didn't have time to talk. And she had to get all dressed up to see her fiancé.

Purse and house, then, were the symbols; but it was clearly marriage that was the source of the freedom. If you were married, even your mother couldn't tell you what to do.

But this wasn't all.

There was yet another version of her that I found as mythic as the one I knew. This was chronicled in a thick flossy-white album that I used to drag out and pore over every afternoon.

While I guess I had the standard small-girl addiction to Brides, my fascination with *her* as a Bride was of a totally different order. I'd stare for hours at that slender, fair, pink-cheeked, curly-haired, excessively pretty girl in the hundred or so manifestations that appeared in the album. Stepping Out The Door From Home. Getting Into The Hire Car. Getting Out Of The Hire Car. Going Into The Church. Signing The Regist-airy. Coming Out Of The Church. Lining Up At The Door Of The Reception. With Mum And Dad And Doug's Mum And Dad. With My Bridesmaids — the pink one ('Janelle, that I went to school with, who's married herself now, with two dear little girls'); the blue one ('Doug's sister Claudie, ditto, but twin boys'); the mauve one ('Glynis, my cousin, same goes for her, except she's got one of each'); and finally, 'Kaylene, my other cousin', the yellow nylon flower girl of whom I was so terribly jealous.

'Why don't you get married again so *I* can be your flower girl?'

'Well ... Doug mightn't be too happy about *that!*'

And we'd both laugh our heads off!

There was also Cutting The Cake. Throwing The Bouquet. The Bridal Waltz. She wasn't really taller than Doug, but looked it in that one.

'How come?' I always asked her.

'I suppose it was the shoes ...'

'But then ...' (Searching for a comparison. Doug didn't actually feature much in the album, which was only right, for he didn't feature much in my vision of her life.) ' ... Then how come you don't look taller in this other one?'

'I dunno, love. Maybe I'd took my shoes off by that time of the night.'

'Can't you remember?' It seemed to me quite incredible that someone could forget the slightest detail of her own wedding.

'It was a long time ago, love.'

'How long?'

'Long enough.' And she would rearrange herself on the bed, or plump up the pillows. The radio would be playing softly and I'd be up the foot-end, facing her, the album on my crossed knees as I barraged her with questions and comments. The fact that I didn't know any of these people — for not only were we not related, but her family came from fifty miles or so inland — added to the curious interest of the album.

'Who's the skinny man in the suit, next to the lady in

the yukky purple?'

And without even checking the illustration, she could tell me.

'Doug's funny-looking, isn't he?' I'd say. 'He's treading on your dress!'

And so we went on, afternoon upon afternoon, through the holidays of a whole summer. We'd also have maybe a little sleep, and she'd smoke and read *True Confessions,* and then Doug would finally slide in and say 'How're my girls?' and she'd get up and put Spam and bread and sauce and stuff on the verandah table and we'd listen to the news and then the repeat of 'Blue Hills'.

When it was dark at last she'd tell him that his girls were very hot and he'd drive us to the beach and we'd dance holding hands in the black night sea, while Doug tactfully went off and had beers with his boring mates at the boring pub. She was too fat for a costume so she tucked her skirt (she wore an old dress for these excursions) into her pants. Her thighs were white and shiny and mine were skinny and brown. Some nights she'd duck right under, clothes and all. Her skirt would fill with air, and balloon right up in front of her.

Then it was the day a letter arrived. Postie delivered it at lunchtime but she just scrutinised the handwriting, and dropped it amongst the litter of out-of-date magazines and half-filled-in crosswords on the table.

'Aren't you going to open it?'

'It's only from Auntie Beryl.'

'Who's she?'

'You know the lady in purple ...?'

'Next to the little skinny man in the suit?'

'Yeah, well that's Auntie Beryl.'

I knew now where she fitted in the arcana. 'That's Kaylene's mum,' I volunteered. 'Auntie Beryl's married to Uncle Eric, and they live out of Dorrigo and run pigs. Or try to. And their little girl is called Kaylene.' Of course, Kaylene was the one I was so jealous of.

She laughed. 'Hardly a little girl any more. She was married herself, last Easter.'

'Kaylene! But she's only my age!'

'She *was*, when the photos were taken ...'

I screwed up my eyes and tried to superimpose the face of Kaylene on to the Bride figure of *her*. But it just looked like a nine year old playing dress-ups. Even more impossible to plant my own skinny mug with its pudding-basin haircut and uneven front teeth on to that symphony of white, that drifting tulle, that sweetheart neckline ...

So I watched instead as she ate beetroot from the tin with her fingers, slice by slice, and then upended the tin itself into her mouth so that the sweet/sour purple juice poured down her throat. Then she lit a Craven A, and ashed into the beetroot tin.

The letter was still on the verandah table that night as she and Doug and I sat drinking tea and waiting for it to be dark enough to go to the beach.

'Aren't you going to open it?' asked Doug, as I had.

'It's only from Auntie Beryl,' she repeated, but this time lazily picked it up, pried open the envelope, started to read the highlights out loud. 'It's hot as Hades there too, she says ... if only the drought would break, she reckons ... The bloke who's got the dairy next door has gone bust and sold up, so Eric's finding it hard to get skim milk for the pigs ... Even their house cow has gone dry ... But now for the good news, says Auntie Beryl. Kaylene and new hubby are very happy and guess what? Kaylene is ...'

A moan seemed to pierce the still night air, and she was off, down the verandah steps and into the backyard, where her nightie flapped like a vast pinky-white moth through the dusk. The letter fluttered to the verandah floor.

Of course at first I thought she'd been caught short, had had to make a sudden dash for the dunny, but she didn't head straight down the path to the outhouse but zotted back and forth across the yard, moaning softly,

'Oh ... oh ... oh ...' As she passed close to the verandah I saw that her hands were beating at her breasts.

Doug picked up the letter, but didn't bother to read it. He laid it gently on the table and went into the kitchen to get a beer.

'Is Kaylene dead?' I wondered. Though how could that be: Auntie Beryl had said it was good news. I sneaked a peak at the letter, managed to spell out the meaning from Auntie Beryl's irregular handwriting. *Kaylene is already expecting.*

Expecting. I knew that was the polite grown-up way of saying pregnant. That was real bad, to be pregnant if you weren't married. My mother was always warning me. It was called Getting Into Trouble. But now the mystery deepened. Kaylene *was* married. She was married last Easter. So why all the fuss and bother? Especially when Auntie Beryl and Uncle Eric were tickled pink about it (I read on further), and Kaylene's hubby Wayne was over the moon ...

'Leave her,' Doug said to me, coming back with his beer, 'she'll get over it in a while.' But he'd no sooner had a sip than he got up again and went down the steps to the yard and then her white fluttering eventually stopped as he led her down through the darkness and they disappeared behind the dead passionfruit vine that clung to the old trellis in front of the incinerator.

There was murmuring for a long time, then silence, a long sniff, and after more silence he led her back by the hand, and settled her in her chair and made a new pot of tea.

Pouring, he suggested a couple of rounds of euchre to cheer us all up.

She smiled bravely. 'You two go on. I'll just watch tonight.'

As there were only the two of us, I persuaded Doug to play cheat instead. He let me shuffle and be dealer, and I cheated my head off, but somehow game after game he still ended up the winner. Then I caught him cheating in reverse — pretending that he *didn't* have cards, in order to let *me* win. That infuriated me even more. I wasn't a baby!

Looking back, I think I must have forgotten that I wasn't in my own family, wasn't with my brothers, for I reached out and punched him on the shoulder muscle.

Doug laughed. 'Looking for a fight are you?' And he tipped me back on my arm, ever so lightly.

I punched hard.

Doug tipped.

I punched hard. I was out of my chair now, flailing at this man who was not even a relative, just a bloke who used to work for Dad on the farm before my eldest brother got old enough to leave school.

Punch.

Tip.

Punch.

Doug was still sitting but had turned around to face me as I danced like a boxer, beating at his chest with both fists. He was grinning wildly and looking to *her,* as if in the hope (I think now) that this game would distract her from the deep silence she had sunk into.

It seemed however to make no impression on her, and after a while he must have tired of it, for he rose and gently pushed me down onto the old cane lounge that sagged against the verandah wall, and then held my wrists together with one of his huge hands, and held my ankles (for I'd started kicking too) with the other.

'I wish you'd drop dead!' I screamed at him.

Instantly, she broke from her torpor in the way that a mother animal will turn if you threaten her young one. *'That's a terrible thing to say!'* And moving at a speed that was absolutely uncharacteristic of her she disappeared into the kitchen, letting the screen door slam behind her. It reverberated on its spring hinge.

That she should come to his defence! And against me! This absolutely shattered the sense of female alliance that I had believed to exist between us, and I couldn't feel the same about her any more.

I cried for a long time that night, and the next

morning before she got up I snuck down to the post office and rang my mother, and that afternoon I went home.

I only saw her twice after that, and the way I saw her on the first subsequent occasion would have shocked me, if I hadn't already had my myth of her independence ruined.

It would have been a year later. It was summer again, and we sat in the lounge — I'd never sat there before. There was her, my mother, me, and my three younger brothers. She wore a proper dress, and stockings, and bone-coloured shoes with small heels and backstraps. (Her feet were too fat to fit into shoes with sides, and even spilled out over the edges of these ones.) She had powder and lipstick on, and she wasn't smoking. Indeed, there wasn't even an ashtray in sight and my mother had to ask for one, very apologetic. 'Does the smoke bother you, dear? I know how I felt when I was.'

She laughed then in almost her old fashion and her fat heaved in the way I'd loved. 'Go right ahead and I'll sniff in the smell of it. I only don't because Doug thinks I shouldn't now.' She added, 'I'm fine, really I am.'

My mother smiled, but her mouth looked as if she'd stuck sticky-tape across it, and she put her cigarette back in the packet. 'Get off her lap!' she suddenly yelled at my littlest brother. 'Auntie doesn't want a great lump like you all over her.' She wasn't our aunt of course, but Mum made the little kids call her that.

'Oh, he's all right,' she said lazily. 'It's all good practice.' But she pushed him off and smoothed her dress down over her stomach.

So I knew then, and teased the boys with my secret as soon as we got home.

We moved to the city shortly afterwards — perhaps that was a farewell visit — and the next time I heard her name was when a real aunt came down to stay at our place because the uncle's bull was going in the Easter Show. On the first afternoon there was a long mumbled conversation in the kitchen between my mother and my aunt, of the kind that my father called Women's Business. I played patience on the passageway floor and listened, but I couldn't get the full gist.

'The same as the last time?' Mum said, shaking her head.

'The same as the last time,' my aunt gloomily agreed.

I yanked my second-littlest brother in from the yard and got him to ask: 'When is that fat auntie going to have her baby?'

'Don't be a silly billy!' Mum and my real aunt put on laughs. 'She isn't having a baby. How on earth did you get that idea in your funny old noggin?' And Mum ruffled his crewcut and gave him the middle bit of the chelsea bun.

'Little pitchers,' my aunt said, and stared nastily in my direction. I wasn't offered any bun at all.

By the time of her third failure I was allowed to hang around Women's Business — presumably in the hope that hearing about tubes and ruptions would turn me off Getting Into Trouble. But though I was privileged now with listening status, I was meant to keep my mouth shut. However, Mum and my aunt were so mysterious on this particular occasion that I just had to say, 'What happened to the baby?'

Mum looked solemn. 'I'm afraid she lost it.'

Lost. For a wild moment I felt a giggle start to rise as my mind made pictures of her losing a baby in the way that I lost my hairbrush, my homework diary, my school hat, every morning of the week. Or perhaps as I lost Scrap the cat sometimes, and would call her around the street at night. 'Scrap, here Scrap ... here puss puss puss ...' At the same time of course I was old enough to know that 'lost' was polite grown-up talk for 'dead', like 'expecting' for 'pregnant'.

But even then I couldn't get a handle on it. 'How come?'

'It was stillborn,' Mum said. 'Just like the last two.'

Still. Born.

Born. Still.

'You mean it came out dead?'

'That's one way of putting it.' Mum pulled a terrible face.

My aunt said, 'Don't they give you homework, in the city?'

I heard nothing about her for a long time after that. Our aunt didn't come down any more because her husband started having trouble with the farm.

('Bloody dairy farmers!' my father would complain. 'When will they learn that it's just not *viable*?' When he'd realised it wasn't viable he'd come to the city to start an equally unviable milk run. 'The money's at the other end,' he used to say when he was struggling with the farm. Now he said, 'There's no money for the small bloke, no matter where he is.')

And so I didn't hear of her, and I almost forgot her, and then we 'dropped in' to the town 'on our way back' from a fortnight's beach holiday when I was fourteen. It wasn't really dropping in, because we stayed three days. And it wasn't really on our way back, because the town was eighty miles north of where we'd holidayed. But that was what they called it, that torture that made me leave the camping ground three days early, when I had just met a boy who had promised to teach me to swim under water. He had a snorkel, and fins, and everything.

It was on the last day that we went to see them, Doug and her. They'd moved too. Doug was now renting a banana plantation up along the coast a bit. He'd had it a couple of years, and it wasn't doing too well. ('Doug's mad,' Dad said. 'He can't beat the bloody combines! There's no hope for the small bloke these days. It's not viable.')

We got there around eleven. 'We'll just drop in for a quick cuppa on our way through,' Mum had said to Doug when she'd rung that morning. The 'quick cuppa' was another of the fictions of that three-day return. I'd sit picking my sunburn through endless hours of talking and tea-drinking, as every single birth, death and marriage that had occurred in the district was annotated. No one of course ever asked if *we* had any news: country people think city slickers don't ever do anything.

'We won't stay for lunch,' Mum had insisted, 'it's too hot for her to fuss. Tell her just a cuppa and a bit of a natter will do us fine.'

We had the cuppa but not the natter, at least not with her, at the two-roomed fibro house at the top of the hill. We sat on the verandah. From there the view swept down through the banana stools that grew in their straight green lines like tropical schoolgirls, their bunches neatly wrapped in bags of blue plastic as if they were breasts or something, something shameful.

'Just can't seem to keep the weeds down,' Doug apologised, seeing Dad eyeing the mess of green that broke through the black-red earth between the rows. 'She should be here soon,' he added, even more apologetically.

The tea was strong even for country tea and my little brothers started whingeing for lemonade until Dad yelled at them.

'There's not even cordial, I'm afraid,' Doug said. 'We don't get kids here often.'

'What the children would really like,' Mum gushed, 'is just fresh country rainwater from the tank! That's the thing I miss most, in the city.' But she had tea herself, and when Doug brought the water out in a cracked plastic jug it was lukewarm and had floating specks of algae in it.

'I've changed my mind and I'll have tea,' I said, swishing my water out over the verandah rail and getting a look from Mum.

Doug poured slowly, to make the time last.

'She's usually back by this time,' he said again.

'She goes for walks,' he told us for the third time. 'There's nothing much else for her to do here, I guess.'

WOMEN'S BUSINESS

In the country when you go for morning tea there are always plates of sandwiches and scones, rock cakes and Anzacs, a boiled fruit cake and a three-layered sponge, and — if you're lucky — lamingtons as well. Here there were plain Saos and stale Arrowroots straight out of the packet, but Mum ate a lot even though at everyone else's place she'd reckoned she was on a diet. The second cup of tea was even stronger than the first, and there was no milk left. It'd been condensed, from a tin.

'That's right, mate,' Dad joked to Doug. 'Don't let the milko fleece the shirt off your back.' And then he stopped laughing quickly when Mum glanced at him, because it certainly looked as if *something* was fleecing the shirt off Doug.

'I told her you were coming,' Doug replied, 'but she doesn't wear a watch of course.'

'Of course not!' Dad agreed, as if wearing a watch was like voting Labor or something.

'She usually just goes for a bit of a stroll ... to get some air ... it gets hot as blazes ...'

'There's a nice breeze up here, anyway,' Mum said, fanning herself with her hand.

'And she just goes down to the south edge of the place,' Doug went on, as if he hadn't heard Mum, 'where it runs into that no-man's-land bit that the Council keeps on reckoning it's going to clear out, and doesn't.'

'Councils!' Dad said.

'Have another biscuit,' Doug said.

'They're lovely and fresh,' Mum said. But she didn't take another.

At last there wasn't any more tea. Doug said he could make up a fresh pot, no sweat, but Mum looked at her watch and said, 'We must really.'

'Must get on the road,' Dad agreed.

'One for the road, then,' Doug joked.

'Twist my arm,' Dad joked back, but we all stood up.

'She'll be real sorry to have missed you,' Doug apologised as we went through the manoeuvre of getting into the car in accordance with our complicated roster of window-sharing. This time it was my turn to squash into the back section of the station wagon, along with the camping gear that didn't fit into the trailer.

'She needs to see people more, that's her trouble,' Doug went on. 'I sometimes think she misses the Bright Lights of town, stuck up here in the sticks.'

(Bright lights of that town! What a joke, I silently mocked.)

'Never mind,' Mum said out the window. 'There's always next time.'

'Sure to be passing through again some time soon,' Dad agreed. He was already starting the engine.

'Bring her down to the Big Smoke for a holiday,' Mum

said. We had to call the city that when we talked to country people. It made them think we didn't like it. 'We can always make up the Nite'n'day in the lounge.'

'Or you can have Little Miss Smarty-pants's room, and she can bunk in with the kids.'

'I might just do that,' Doug called after us as we started down the track. 'I might just do that!'

He never did of course, and it was on that day that I saw her for the last time. The others didn't, not even Mum or Dad: it was only because I was sitting where I was, looking out the back of the station wagon ...

We were nearly down to the road, and the track had veered right over to the south. In that place the banana stools had gone wild, sprouting in great clumps with creepers tangling through and around them. The broad leaves were yellow-brown at the edges and the few bunches that had managed to grow were small, the fruit tiny, wizened, and going black on the stalk. I could hardly make her out at first for she was like a large, translucent, pink jellyfish breaststroking slowly just beneath the surface of a thick green pool of algae. Vines hung around her, great cords with darkened leaves, and as she sank and surfaced back and forth behind this curtain of black-green, her body soft and floating as if it was weightless, I remembered how she'd looked when she had struggled through the bright plastic fly-screen with the loaf of warm bread that she immediately broke in two, and then I thought of Trevor MacKenzie, his arrow-body shooting through the clear waters of the lagoon, and I found myself collapsing into one of those unaccountable fits of the giggles that you get when you're a girl of fourteen.

MELTING POINT

translation: n. (1) The process of turning something (written or spoken) from one language into another; also, the product of this. (2) Transformation, alteration, change. (3) The act of being carried or conveyed to heaven without death.

I can't bear it any fucking longer. Sometimes I feel as if I'll go crazy, start throwing things, climb up the wall, lose it completely (or just pack my bag and split from home) if ever again in my life I hear Yaya going on and on like a scratchy old record:

> 'Stin Kríti ta koritsákia.
> 'Stin Kríti ta koritsákia.
> 'Stin Kríti ta koritsákia.'
> *In Crete the young maidens ...*

Who gives a shit about what the maidens did on the island of Crete in the land of Greece in the dim dark days of ancient history? This is Newtown, New South Wales, Australia, in the last decade of the twentieth century, and I am an Australian girl — second generation, if you must know — even if I do have a crazy name like Xenia Hadzithakis.

So there!

'Daedalus interea Creten logumque perosus exilium tactusque loci natalis amore clausus erat pelago ...' Xenia announces, then moves straight into a fluent translation:

'Meanwhile Daedalus, hating Crete and his long exile, and homesick for his birthplace, was shut in by the sea.' Xenia smiles towards the front desk.

'Excellent!' Ms Boot declares. 'Congratulations to all three of you.'

'Three ...?' Xenia glances around the classroom. At the best of times there are only two students in the Year 11 Latin class, and Nguyen Tuyet Nhung is at choir practice today.

'Yes, three,' Ms Boot replies. 'Publius Ovidus Naso, known as Ovid, who wrote the *Metamorphoses* — meaning *Changes* — in the cities of Rome and Tomis during the reign of the Emperor Augustus in the first couple of decades Anno Domini; Professor Evelyn J. Douglas who produced the Student Classics translation at a Scottish university town in the late 1950s ...'

Xenia uncomfortably shifts the paperback on her knees.

'And you, Xenia Hadzithakis,' Ms Boot goes on, 'of Chisholm Girls' High School, valiantly labouring away at Latin literature in the double period before lunch on the Monday of the third week of the month named for Augustus in the Year of Indigenous People, 1993.'

'Beats me as to why,' Ms Boot adds, ' but I guess you have your reasons.'

Yes and no. At first I did it because the alternatives on the timetable were art, which I'm no good at, and physics, which I hate. And then by the end of last year, when it was time to choose HSC subjects, I'd realised I quite like it.

NOT that I'd ever let on to anyone. It doesn't exactly go with my image.

Wild Xenia. Party girl.

OUTRAGEOUS.

Xenia defying the school uniform policy with her black fishnet tights, black army boots painted with silver stars and moons, black velvet mini-skirt barely covering her bum, black singlet over bare Xenia, and loops and loops of silver chains that are so groovy, where'd you get them, Xenia? (Secret: they're from the plumbing shop that Dad gets his supplies at. Meant to be for flushing those old-fashioned dunnies.)

Xenia who is always the first to answer back, argue the point, stand up to any teacher. The Principal included.

Xenia who was the first one in the class to have sex with a boy.

And the first to say that all the blokes she knows are meatheads and until a decent one comes along she isn't going to do it any more.

Xenia who smokes dope, drinks bourbon and coke, knowing exactly how much she can handle, never but NEVER getting out of control.

Xenia who has the best ideas for places to hold parties, like last year at Halloween in the Newtown Cemetery.

Xenia who always knows where to go to listen to the newest bands before anyone else has even heard of them.

Xenia who is just sooooooooooo cooooooooooooooooool ...

So how come she does Latin?

Secret: despite the crib on my lap, I like translating. For its own sake. Doesn't matter what the text is about, I just like (when I'm in the mood; I'm not today) puzzling out the meaning. Like some people are jigsaw fanatics:

they don't care what it's a picture of, they just like the challenge of the puzzle.

Add to this the fact that my family disapprove of me doing Latin.

(Dad: Why don't you learn physics, go to university and become a scientist?)

(Mum: Why don't you learn art, go to tech, become a clothes designer?)

(Yaya: Why don't you learn Ancient Greek, or proper modern Greek, not this Aussie-slang Greek that you speak, fit only for barbarians?)

'*"Terras licet"* inquit *"et undas obstruat, et caelum certe patet; ibimus illac: omnia possideat, non possidet aera Minos",'* says Ms Boot.

Huh?

'Concentrate please, Xenia. I was merely reading to you the next passage for translation: "Then he — that's Daedalus — said: "Though he — that's the king — can block our escape by land or by sea, surely the sky is open. We shall go that way. Minos may possess everything, but he does not possess the air."' Ms Boot gave Xenia a questioning look. 'You are familiar with the background to the story of Daedalus, I take it?'

'Kind of.'

'Recap, please. We only spent all last week on it.'

'Well, Daedalus was this sort of inventor bloke, and he went to Crete and he built this maze called the labyrinth, so that the king — his name was Minos — could imprison this monster, who was called the Minotaur, that the king's wife had given birth to after screwing with a bull. Jeez, Miss, imagine...'

Ms Boot doesn't blink. 'Excellent summary, if somewhat colloquially expressed. And so we have now reached the point at which Daedalus is sick of Crete —'

('I don't blame him. Sounds deadly, if you ask me.')

'What was that, Xenia?'

'Nothing, Miss.'

'Daedalus is tired of his exile — Xenia, who else do we know who was suffering exile?'

(*My Yaya.* Stop it.) 'Ovid, Miss. When he was halfway through writing the *Metamorphoses* he was exiled by the Emperor Augustus, and had to go and live at this awful place called Tomis on the Black Sea.'

'Very good. And so when Ovid writes of the exile of Daedalus, we can imagine that he does so with a certain personal feeling. But to continue — at this stage of the story, Daedalus is homesick and tired of his exile, and he laments the fact that there is no escape by land or sea. And so what does he do?'

'Catches an aeroplane?'

'You've obviously read this before, Xenia.' Ms Boot

looks down over her reading specs.

'Just joking, Miss.'

'No, but you're right. Daedalus, the great inventor, proceeded to discover a way of flying. He set his mind — Ovid tells us — he set his mind to sciences that had never been explored before, and he changed the laws of nature.'

Ms Boot's voice is so strong, so convincing, that for a moment Xenia is taken in.

'Truly?'

And then she realises. She is pleased Nguyen Tuyet Nhung wasn't here to see her idiocy. For how could someone have invented a way of flying in — what? — a couple of thousand years BC? Apart from the fact that this is a myth anyway: believing in Daedalus would be like believing in the Tooth Fairy.

'Just think of it as science fiction, Xenia. Oh yes, as well as Evelyn J. Douglas under the desk I have watched you over the years with a variety of sf, going from bug-eyed monsters in your early years to this punk-whatsummy stuff you're into now.'

'Cyber-punk,' Xenia says enthusiastically. 'William Gibson. Did you know he wrote this novel on computer disc, and there were only ten or something copies of it in the world, and as the people who bought it read it, it self-destructed?'

'Sounds totally elitist to me. One assumes that those ten discs sold for a fortune. And pointless. If you only want ten readers in the world, you'd do better to join a creative writing collective. No, give me old Publius Ovidus Naso any day. To write something that lasts for two thousand years — now *that* is science fiction, *that* is defying the laws of time.' Ms Boot pulls herself up short, gives Xenia a shrewd look.

'But if you think you are successfully diverting me, Madam, away from the subject at hand, you've another think coming. This is double period Latin. I have written in my term schedule that Year 11 will spend this time translating Ovid's *Metamorphoses*, Book VIII, lines 183 to 235: the story of Daedalus and Icarus. I have also written that I myself shall spend this time correcting all the Year 8 homework in preparation for my class with them this afternoon. So if you will kindly hand me Professor Douglas's translation from your lap, you will be able to begin the task in hand.'

Xenia shoots her a painful look. Sometimes, when Nhung is at choir, she and Ms Boot spend the whole lesson discussing stuff like the political influence of prostitutes in Periclean Athens, the importance of homosexuality in Alexander the Great's army, grisly murders amongst the later Augustan emperors, whether lead poisoning was really responsible for the decline of the Roman Empire, and favourite bits in the novels of Robert Graves and Mary Renault.

But not today, obviously.

Ms Boot pulls a face and opens the first of a huge pile of exercise books. Then relenting slightly, she offers, 'I'll start you off, Xenia.'

'*Nam ponit in ordine pennas* ... He — Daedalus — put the feathers in a row, *a minima coeptas, longam breuiore sequenti*, beginning with the shortest and placing a long one next to a short one, *ut clivo crevisse putes*, so that you would imagine they had grown upon a slope ...' Ms Boot firmly shuts her own Ovid, replaces it with a copy of the Year 8 text. 'Now you are on your own ...'

But the words are jangling on the page, the anger inside me is screaming, my eyes are still washed out from holding back the tears of fury (wouldn't do for the famous Xenia to arrive at school with mascara weeping down her cheeks), my stomach is churning with the after-effects of all that hatred, plus perhaps sheer hunger, for amongst the drama I somehow neglected to cram down a bowl of muesli, a piece of Vegemite toast.

This morning was indescribable.

The *worst* fight.

Get this: I am in the bathroom putting on my make-up and she goes: *Blah blah blah blah* about my skirt, my tights, my singlet, my boots, my chains, my earrings, my sexual behaviour ...

Oh yeah, she puts on this act about how she doesn't speaka da Ingliss but she knows everything, no worries, she just sums me up with her eyes. She knows, and I know she knows, and she knows I know she knows, and ...

See what I mean?

She's like that labyrinth that Daedalus made — she gets you in, you can't ever get out again.

Dad says that in Greece they sometimes call the old women *'Gorgónes'*. Gorgons. Like those ladies with snakes for hair in the myths. If you even looked at them, you got turned to stone.

They've got the power to put the Evil Eye on you, you know. Women like my grandmother. True. Or that's what the Greeks reckon.

Where was I?

So this morning in the bathroom she goes: *Blah blah blah blah Madonna.*

Like she's saying I am trying to look like Madonna.

I hate Madonna. I despise Madonna. I grew out of Madonna years ago.

But yeah okay, I suppose if I have to look at my style, I

have to admit that there are influences of Madonna. But who wants to go analysing her style at 7.30 a.m. in the bathroom mirror?

And then the chorus cuts in: *'Stin Kríti ta koritsákia then parasténoun ti Madonna.'*

Subtitle: In Crete, the young maidens don't model themselves upon Madonna.

I'll bet they don't.

They're dags, those Cretan maidens.

Where was I?

Better get down to it.

I can feel Ms Boot eyeballing me over the pile of homework.

Tum lino medias et ceris alligat imas
atque ita compositas paruo curuamine flectit
ut ueras imitetur aues.

Tum lino medias	with thread the middle
et ceris	and wax
alligat imas	he bound together the base
atque ita compositas	and when they were so composed
paruo curuamine flectit	he bent to a little curve
ut ueras imitetur aue	in order that they would imitate true birds

Then Daedalus joined (the feathers) together at the centre and base with thread and with wax. And when he had arranged them like this, he bent them round into a gentle curve, so that they would look like (the wings of) real birds.

Puer Icarus una stabat
The boy Icarus was standing with him.

The boy Icarus ...
     How old was he?
     Ovid goes on about Daedalus being homesick, but what about Icarus?

I went on a Brownie camp once, but in the middle of the first night I woke up and I cried so much that Brown Owl had to ring up Dad to come and get me. Yaya came with him too, in the middle of the night. And took me home.

That night in the car I sat in the back seat with her, and she sang lullabies. But I was restless as always, wanted talk not soothing, so she told me the story of her own homesickness ...

Subtitle: Once upon a time and a long time ago, I left my homeland, my native village of Tria Platania and my island of Kriti, and I travelled far away on a boat, and I didn't know where I was going. My father had arranged with my godfather that I would go to a place called Sythney, Afstralia, and I would marry another godchild of my godfather, who had migrated to that foreign place. His name was Nikos Hadzithakis. And so I went. I was seventeen years old. The year was 1949. And so I went.

'And what happened?' I asked, in the darkness of the car.

'Well, I married him. As your father is the proof. And I made my life here.'

I was just a Brownie guide, seven maybe, with my flanelette jamies on under a tracksuit, and the enormousness of what Yaya was saying was too much for me to take in. I said: 'Were you sad?'

'Popopopopo,' my yaya exclaimed. *'Vevéos! Asfalós!* Truly! Indeed! Was I sad! I was homesick every minute of every living day, but that was my life and I made it.'

As to Icarus, I think of him now, feeling out of place in Crete, where the Greek they speak is different and the other kids tease him. I think I am starting to get a handle on all this. (But in my version, Icarus is seventeen, like me.)

THE NIGHT TOLKIEN DIED

Puer Icarus una
stabat et, ignarus sua se tractare pericla,
ore renidenti modo, quas uaga mouerat aura,
captabat plumas, flauam modo pollice ceram
mollibat lusuque suo mirabile patris
impediebat opus.

His son Icarus was standing nearby and, not realising that he was handling his own danger, his face shone as he caught at the feathers which the breeze was blowing about. And he was softening the yellow wax with his thumb, and he was interrupting his father's miraculous work by his game.

Talking of miraculous, it is incredible how much better I am starting to feel, after doing just that much translation. It really works for me like doing a crossword soothes my mum, or woodwork calms my dad down — or I guess crochet helps my yaya settle herself, after a storm. This morning her hooked needle was bobbing in and out as fast a machine.

I used to love that, when I was a kid. Watching her crochet, or sew, or spin the long hanks of raw wool that she would buy. As she'd work, she'd sing softly under her breath the words of the *mantinádes* that she had sung when she was a girl, she said.

'Otan ímouna koritsáki stin Kríti ...' When I was a girl

in Crete ...

It didn't give me the shits in those days, to be hearing about her growing up in Greece. Actually, I used to like it, used to beg her for stories.

'*Yaya, pes mou éna paramýthi,*' I would beg. Yaya, tell me a story.

'*Tha sou po ena paramýthi...*' she would sometimes begin. I will tell you a fairytale ...

'*Embrós,*' I'd urge. '*Pes to.*' Go on. Tell it.

'*To kookí ke to revithi ...*' About the broad bean and the chick pea ...

'A broad bean and a chick pea!' I would exclaim. 'What happened to them?'

She would grin her wicked grin to tease me (the same grin that drives me crazy now).

'*Ke zísane aftí kalá, ki emís kalítera ...*' she would announce, meaning: They lived well but we live better. That was the way the stories always ended.

'Oh Yaya, that's not fair,' I'd complain at her trick. And I would beg her to tell me a real story — one of the Red Thread yarns, perhaps, which are the traditional Greek folk tales, or a real-life story about how when she was growing up, it was the time of the Second World War and the Nazis were occupying Crete, and she and her friends used to take food to some Australian soldiers who were hiding in a cave in the mountains. On more than one occasion, they had to run for their lives to escape from patrols of Nazi soldiers!

It sounded so exciting, compared to me and my friends playing with our Barbie dolls under the rotary clothesline.

So when was it that I started to get sick of the stories (sick of her)?

I can't exactly remember the first fight, but I must have been in Year 7. That's when I started hitching up the skirt of my school uniform, drawing lines around my eyes with a 6B pencil, making earrings out of safety pins and ring-pulls ...

That's when I started answering back.

(Like this morning. What I said. Stop it.)

postquam manus ultima coepto
imposita est, geminas opifex librauit in alas
ipse suum corpus motaque pependit in aura.
After he had put the finishing touches to what he had started, the inventor balanced his own body on a pair of wings and hung poised in the air currents.

instruit et natum 'medio' que 'ut limite curras,
Icare,' ait 'moneo, ne, si demissior ibis,
unda grauet pennas, si celsior, ignis adurat':

MELTING POINT

He instructed his son too, and he said, 'I warn you, Icarus, to fly a middle course. Otherwise, if you go too low, the water may weigh down your wings, and if you fly too high, the sun's fire may burn them.'

Sounds like the sort of thing my other grandmother says to me. Mum's mum, I mean. I call her Nanna. She's a dinky-di Aussie, through and through, she says, looking sideways at Dad, who was born here but of course has a Greek name, and looking even more sideways at Yaya, who looks like she could have stepped off the migrant ship five minutes, rather than forty-four years, ago.

(Dad always reckons Yaya is a walking advertisement for the failure of the Australian government's assimilation policy. That was the official attitude to migrants when Yaya came out here: they were expected to give up their own cultures and 'assimilate' into Anglo society. Sounds like throwing a whole lot of different ingredients into a pot and turning up the heat till everything melts into a big gluggy mess.)

But where was I?

Oh yes, Nanna and the middle course. She's always saying to me, 'Don't set your sights too high, my girl. Don't get above yourself.' She tells me that an apprenticeship was good enough for my father, and business college for my mother, so why do I think I'm so special, that I should want to go to university and study linguistics?

One of Nanna's terms of abuse for people (apart from 'New Australian', 'Immigrant', 'Refugee' and 'Ethnic') is 'High Flyer'. She'll say of anyone from the new parish priest to the Prime Minister, 'He'd be okay I s'pose, if it wasn't that he's a real high flyer.'

I remember once she said it when we were watching an interview on TV with the leader of the Red Devils squad of stunt pilots. 'Look at him! Thinks he's just it! Talk about a real high flyer!'

Yaya knows a bloody sight more Ingliss than she makes out. (After twenty years of working in a shop you have to be able to talk to people; it is just that, now she's retired, she mostly chooses not to.) On this occasion, she caught my eye and started giggling. 'Well, he wouldn't want to be a *low* flyer,' she murmured as the TV screen showed the scarlet stunt plane looping the loop, 'or he'd end up in somebody's lounge room.'

One thing I have to say for Yaya, she might put me down all the time, for how I look and how I act, but she never puts me down like Nanna does. Quite the opposite in fact. Whenever I show her anything — whether it's a cake I've made or a school report with straight As — she always lifts her eyes to heaven and sniffs and says, 'What is all the fuss about? You are capable of far more than that!' And when I was a little girl she used to tell me she was looking forward to the day when I would be Australia's first woman prime minister. Truly!

    Where was I?

'inter utrumque uola, nec te spectare Booten
aut Helicen iubeo strictumque Orionis ensem;
me duce carpe uiam.' pariter praecepta uolandi
tradit et ignotas umeris accomodat alas.
inter opus monitusque genae maduere seniles
et patriae tremuere manus. dedit oscula nato
non iterum repetenda suo pennisque leuatus
ante uolat comitque timet, uelut ales ab alto
quae teneram prolem produxit in aera nido,
hortaturque sequi damnosasque erudit artes.
(et mouet ipse suas et nati respicit alas.)

'Fly between the water and the sun,' (Daedalus told Icarus), 'and — I'm telling you — don't look at [the stars called] Bootes or Helice or the drawn sword of Orion. Just follow my leadership.' At the same time he fitted the unfamiliar wings to Icarus's shoulders, and told him how to fly. While working and talking, the old man's cheeks became wet with tears and his fatherly hands shook. He kissed his son — which he would never do again — and rising up on his wings, he flew off in front. Though he was worrying about his companion like a bird leading its offspring from a high nest into thin air, he encouraged Icarus to follow and taught him the perilous art of flying, flapping his own wings and looking back at his son.

You can just see it, can't you?

A couple of years ago there was a kookaburra nest in the gum tree next door, and every afternoon I would sit in our yard and watch as the parent birds taught the three kids how to fly. Two got the hang of it real quick, but this other bird, he was so stupid — and scared! You could see him tiptoeing down the branch, then screwing up his courage, and then — like someone leaning to dive — doing false start after false start before he'd finally leap off the branch. Mum and Dad would be in front, showing him how, but he'd go flutter flutter flutter flutter, then zoom fall thunk down to the lower branch, where he'd hang on for grim death. (Or is it grim life you're meant to hang on to?)

As the weeks went on, first one and then the next of the teenage kookaburras flew off, never to be seen again, but spring was over well and truly and Number 3 was still a real stick-at-home. You could see his parents were getting so sick of it.

Finally, one afternoon I watched as the first adult zoomed off and away. The other one gave some last-minute instructions, then flap flap flap flap, off it went too, leaving the young bird to follow.

Well! Did he squark, up there alone on his branch. But as the adult was swooping towards the clouds the young one took a deep breath (you could almost feel it yourself) and shut his eyes (I'm sure he shut his eyes) and —

   JUMP
      FLAP
    FLAP FLAP
            FLAPFLApflapflapflapfLAPFLAPFLAP

        and he was off and away ...

This next bit is full of island names: Samos, Delos, Paros, Lebinthos, Kalymnos. I search for them on the map at the front of my Ovid ...

Here they are. Scattered up the right-hand side of the Aegean Sea, towards the coast of Turkey. Of course this map is only black and white, but Yaya has a huge coloured one pinned to her bedroom wall, and as I look now the sea takes on the blue of Yaya's Aegean and I can see the islands below me as I swoop in flight ...

THE NIGHT TOLKIEN DIED

et iam Iunonia laeua
parte Samos (fuerant Delosque Parosque relictae),
dextra Lebinthos erat fecundaque melle Calymne,
cum puer audaci coepit gaudere uolatu
And now they have whizzed over Delos and Paros, leaving them behind towards the left, and Samos — sacred to the goddess Juno — and they can see Lebinthos towards the right, and now Kalymnos, rich in honey. And the boy starts to revel in his bold flight ...

  swooping
    down
      down   up
        down   up
          down   up
            down   up
              hovering
            like and eagle
              hanging
               gliding
              drifting
             wheeling

'Xenia ...' murmurs Ms Boot, 'what on earth are you muttering under your breath?' and Xenia swoops back to her Latin text ...

MELTING POINT

cum puer audaci coepit gaudere uolatu
deseruitque ducem caelique cupidine tractus
altius egit iter.
And the boy
starting to revel in his bold flight
stops following his father and,
drawn by the open sky,
soars higher
          and
                  ever higher ...

OH NO!

rapidi uicinia solis
mollit odoratas, pennarum uincula, ceras.
The closeness of the fiery sun softens the fragrant wax
that holds his wings ...
tabuerant cerae;
The wax melts
              (feathers floating
                      (feathers falling
nudos quatit ille lacertos
remigioque carens non ullas percipit auras
he beats his bare arms up and down
  but without wings they take no hold
upon the air

THE NIGHT TOLKIEN DIED

      (falling
           (falling
                 (falling
                       (falling
                             (falling
                                  (falling

(through blue air white clouds
            flurry of feathers

oraque caerulea patrium clamantia nomen

excipiuntur aqua

and he cries out his father's name again and again

        Daedalus Daedalus
            Dad Dad
              Dad
              Dad

until he is silenced by the dark blue sea.

As the lunch bell rings and tears roll down the face of the famous Xenia Hadzithakis, Ms CooooooooL of the SchooooooooooL herself.

  'My dear child,' says Ms Boot, 'what on earth is the matter?'

  Xenia takes a deep sniff but the tears keep splashing

down on the page of translation which Ms Boot now rescues from the downpour.

'Is it this?' she asks gently. 'The death of Icarus?'

'Yes/no/that and/this morning ...'

This morning what I yelled at Yaya ...

If Crete's so fucking fantastic, why don't you go back to where you come from?

' ...Catharsis,' Ms Boot is saying, rabbitting on to herself about classical literature as she does from time to time. Usually a form of self-indulgence, she knows, but this time it serves to give Xenia a breathing space, the last thing this girl would want is a shoulder to cry on ...

(Why does everyone always think I'm so strong that I don't need a shoulder to cry on? 'Xenia Hadzithakis?' they all say. 'Oh don't worry about her — she's as tough as nails!')

' ...Catharsis,' Ms Boot was saying to the air, 'from the Greek *katharsis.* cf Aristotle's *Poetics,* Book 6 if I remember correctly? The effect of art in purifying the emotions by providing a vicarious experience of tragedy ... hence the phrase "purged by pity and terror" ... Feeling a little more yourself now, Xenia?'

Sniff.

Snap out of this.

Think translation.

Katharsis. Where do I know that word from? Ah — *Kathara Theftera.* Clean Monday. The day after carnival finishes and in Kriti the koritzákia take picnics up to the mountain tops, where they fly kites that carry their sins away to heaven and leave their souls clean and shining as their eyes.

That's what Yaya used to tell me.

Through the last of her tears, Xenia fakes a grin. 'Yeah, Miss. I'm okay. Must've got something in my eye.'

As if to help bring the moment back to ordinary, Xenia's stomach gives a loud rumble.

Ms Boot packs the Year 8 homework books into her bag. 'Sounds to me,' she says, 'as if you need to go and have your lunch.'

Lunch. That stuff you eat in the middle of the day when you're starving.

But in her fury this morning Xenia not only neglected to eat breakfast but she forgot to make her lunch. And in her stormy exit from the house, she also forgot to bring her purse.

She could of course borrow a couple of bucks, go to the tuckshop, but somehow she doesn't feel like seeing the gang yet, not like this with black lines of sorrow weeping down her cheeks. ('Haven't you guys heard? It's the latest! You put on your make-up then you peel a kilo of onions so it all washes down ...' Doesn't sound convincing, Xenia.)

No, what she'll do is find a quiet spot and hole up by herself this lunchtime. Pity about starving to death, but it can't be helped.

Oh yes it can, because standing holding a large cane basket in the middle of the playground is a little black bundle of bones and rags that can only be Xenia Hadzithakis's yaya.

'Ella!' she screeches in a voice to shatter windows, *'Ella, koritsáki mou!'* Come! Come here, my young lady! *'Echo to faí sou! To kséhases! Prépi na fas! Ella, élla!'* I have your lunch! You forgot it! You must eat! Come here, come here!

All the Year Sevens and Year Eights and Year Nines and Year Tens are having a field day — staring, pointing, laughing their heads off at the spectacle of the famous Xenia's granny bringing her lunch to school, just like she was a kindy kid or something. And the uproar is so great that even some Year Elevens and Twelves are peering over the wall from the senior area to see what the fun is.

Talk about EMBARRASSING!

Anyone else would never live it down.

But just get what Xenia does!

She lifts that head of hers high in the air, tosses that

mane of gothic curls and — walking slowly and smiling at her audience like a queen — she crosses the asphalt, kisses her yaya upon the cheek, loops the basket over one arm and puts her other arm around her grandmother, and she leads the old woman to the sacred patch of lawn in front of the principal's office, where no one ever dares to set foot.

There she settles her visitor upon an ornamental rock, and seats herself upon the grass, and proceeds to lay out the contents of the basket upon a clean white napkin for all the world to see.

Fresh crusty bread ...

Stuffed vine leaves, dark and glistening ...

Fat black olives ...

Tiny red tomatoes ...

A hunk of soft white cheese ...

Strips of bright green capsicum and cucumber ...

Two boiled eggs ...

A container of soft pink taramasalata ...

Four oranges ...

A handful of figs ...

And a large bottle of spring water.

'Embrós,' says Yaya, *'as fáme.'* So, let us eat.

And they do.

'A word — if I may interrupt, Xenia?'

It is the principal, in her most sarcastic voice. She is standing on the edge of her lawn, staring at the remnants of the picnic.

Yaya smiles up brightly at her. She's not understanding Ingliss today.

Xenia rises. Goes across to her, yanking the miniskirt perhaps another millimetre down her bum. 'Yes, Miss?'

The dialogue is predictable: what on earth did Xenia think she was doing, sitting on the special lawn et cetera, even if she did have her grandmother visiting, and really, unauthorised persons shouldn't be on school property, though perhaps this once (smiling back in a plastic fashion at Yaya)...

So Xenia is just escaping with the promise that she'll know not to do it next time, Miss, when Miss observes her uniform.

Or lack of such.

Lack of anything very much, if the truth be told.

The heavens unfold again: how dare Xenia wear a black velvet miniskirt, a black singlet over nothing but her own body, these appalling fishnet tights, festoons of chains, and army boots! Who does she think she is — Madonna?

Xenia shrugs. Yes, Miss. No, Miss. Think what you like, Miss. I hear it all at home, all the time, Miss.

But Yaya is on her feet, grinning broadly at the

principal, proudly stroking at the arm of her granddaughter as if to show her off. *'Íne oréo, to koritsáki mou, pára polí oréo?'* She is beautiful, my young maiden, she is very beautiful, isn't she?

The principal gets the gist, despite the language barrier, and knows enough not to insult students in front of relatives who can put the Evil Eye on you.

'Yes, well, perhaps under all that make-up,' she agrees. 'But you are to go home immediately Xenia, and get changed into something more appropriate. I do not want you going around setting a bad example to the younger girls.'

Would you believe it? An afternoon off, with permission!

As the back-to-lessons bell rings, Yaya and Xenia scoot out the gate together, giggling like a couple of truants.

'Ta skolía!' exclaims Yaya. *'Pánta ta misoúsa. Nióthis san to poulí sto klouví!'* Schools! I have always hated them. You feel like a bird in a cage!

'Tell me about it!' Xenia agrees.

'Ke tóra,' says Yaya, *'pou páme?'* And now — where shall we go?

A memory from this morning sparks a brainwave: I KNOW! Then instant deflation: Xenia has no money.

Yaya pulls out her little black purse, shows that there are a couple of twenties in there. 'Is my shout,' she announces in the broadly accented Australian that she uses only on rare occasions these days.

And off they go ...

UP   UP
  and   and   and
    DOWN   DOWN

The waves rock and roll as the Manly ferry surges out past the Heads, with a tall black-clad figure and a tiny black-clad figure standing at the prow. The sea today is dark blue, mirroring the sky, where tiny filaments of cloud drift.

As Xenia looks down, the islands of the map come into her mind, as if she can see them etched beneath her on the waves. And now the picture broadens, and Xenia finds herself realising that, as all the oceans of the world ultimately join together, some of the water here in Sydney Harbour could once have been in that very sea where Icarus fell.

And as a gust of wind whips the sea spray up towards her, Xenia closes her eyes and opens her mouth and tastes the salty blue of the Aegean.

Yaya is asking something, but Xenia cannot hear her for the pounding of the sea.

'*Ti? Ti ípes?*' Xenia yells back at her. What? What did

you say?

'*Tha érthis mazí mou?*' Yaya asks. Would you come with me?

'Where?' Xenia shouts against the wind. 'Come with you where?'

Yaya grins wickedly, but there is longing in her voice as she replies in her broadest Australian, 'If I go back to where I come from ...'

'*Asfalós!*' Xenia agrees. '*Vevéos!*' Of course! Certainly I will. But not just to Kriti, Xenia thinks. I want to go to Samos — sacred to the goddess Juno — and to Delos and to Paros, and to Kalymnos, rich in honey ...

Then Xenia remembers Yaya's tricks of the past, and she gives her grandmother a hard look. 'But if I go with you to Kriti, to meet the relatives, I'm going as I am, okay?' She tosses her head, and half a dozen earrings made of wire and feathers and bottletops tangle together. 'Don't expect me to assimilate!'

'*Entáxi*, Xenia, okay, *íse eléfthero pouli.*' You're free as a bird.

Yaya laughs and slips her arm around her granddaughter's black velvet waist. 'I bet you'll show those Cretan girls a thing or two!'

THE CONVICT BOX

Some of this story is about me, and some of it is about a fictional person. As I'm not absolutely sure where the reality stops and the invention starts, I'll try to put it down just as it happened.

I am sixteen years old and I live in Katoomba, New South Wales, and my name is Dan Baker. (Or it mostly is. But you'll see.) It was last winter when it started (it's the morning of 31 December now) and maybe I should say that last winter was really bad.

I don't mean the weather (though it gets pretty blizzardy up here in the Blue Mountains), but Mum. She was on my back all the time, really getting at me. 'Clean up your room!' 'Turn that music down!' 'Don't leave your skateboard in the passageway!' 'Do the washing up!' 'Put the peanut butter away after you've used it!' 'Pick up your skateboard!' 'Turn that bloody Jimi Hendrix down!' 'Will you clean up your room please, Daniel Baker!'

That was normal. I could cut off from that. But as well as all this usual stuff there was a new track on the record, about how I was in Year 10 and the School Certificate exams were coming up and if I didn't pull my finger out, I wouldn't be able to go on to Year 11, and what would happen to me then? 'It's your future,' she kept saying, 'It's your future, not mine, that's at stake.'

One night we had a really bad blue, and I snapped. 'Yeah, you're right,' I yelled. 'It is *my* future, not yours.' I told her that I didn't want to go on to the HSC anyway.

She got spitting mad then. 'If you think I'm going to have you hanging about the house doing nothing — and you *would* be doing nothing, there's no jobs up here...'

No worries, I told her. I'd go to Perth and live with Dad. Then she'd be free of me for good.

I thought she'd hit the roof, tell me I couldn't, she wouldn't allow me, etc. etc. She's always been a bit funny about me even seeing Dad when he comes across to Sydney for a gig, about once every blue moon. (He's a muso, see, and a bit of a pisspot, and she's scared it might be catching.) But she just said, 'Oh well. If that's what you really want...'

After that, she stopped nagging, but things were somehow worse. I just felt as if she didn't care about me, as if she didn't really want me. She enrolled in this photography course at TAFE, and I heard her telling

THE CONVICT BOX

Nan over the phone that when I moved out she'd turn my room into a darkroom. 'Of course I'll have to get the water put on, take a pipe through the wall from the bathroom. Don't know how the landlord will feel about that ...' It was as if me leaving home was less important than the plumbing.

Funnily enough, now that Mum had stopped going on all the time about homework, I didn't seem to mind it so much. Or maybe it was something to do. There was this awful sort of embarrassed silence between us if I went out into the lounge room to watch TV with her, so I just stayed in my room, most nights.

Anyway, that's all the background. The story really starts one day in about June, when Ms Papadopoulos, that's our history teacher, gave us this assignment. We'd been doing early white settlement, convicts and all that. We'd gone on an excursion out to the old courthouse and gaol at Hartley, near the Coxs River, and we'd looked at this sandstone culvert that the road gangs had built on the Victoria Pass. We'd read photocopies of old documents about living conditions and stuff, and now Ms Pap said: 'I want you to imagine you're a convict, and you've been assigned as a servant to a master in the bush, and all your belongings in the whole world fit in a box the size of a shoebox ...'

So we had to collect all the things for our own convict

box. We had a month to do it in.

That night, over tea, I told Mum about it. I don't know why — I guess it was just something to say. I could see she was really interested — she always watches history documentaries if they're on TV — but she just said, 'Poor things, it must've been so hard for them, leaving their homes ...' And then she bit her tongue, because since the night of the bad blue, we'd avoided any mention of 'going' or 'leaving' or even of 'home'. (I wondered what it'd be like, living four thousand kilometres away in Perth. I mean, the furthest west I've ever been is Dubbo Zoo.)

Of course, with a whole month to collect the convict stuff I put off doing it, but over the next week or so I found myself making little lists in my head, or suddenly thinking of something. I'd be skating with my mates in the car park, and I'd think *'Candle!'* Or I'd be listening to Jimi Hendrix (I do like lots of new stuff too, but he's the best guitarist ever) and I'd think 'A spare bit of boot leather would come in handy ...' And one Saturday, when it was too wet to go out, I went to the garage to oil the bearings on my skateboard, and I found myself picking through the shelf of old stuff that years and years of previous tenants had left — bits of wire, all sizes of nails, a huge old bolt, a piece of dog chain, a rusty tobacco tin, three fish hooks ... If you'd been sent halfway across the world with nothing, then stuff like that would probably seem like treasure.

Mum came in then, to get the blockbuster (we've got a fuel stove as well as the electric one). I thought she was going to tell me to split some wood, but she just said, 'You'd probably have to cook for yourself, you know.'

Huh? Dad was on the move a lot, the band did country gigs as well as city pubs. I guess I'd kind of imagined that I'd travel round with him, but I suppose (I thought when Mum said that) I suppose he wouldn't always have room in the van for me, and I'd sometimes have to stay by myself in the flat in Perth. 'No worries,' I told Mum. 'I'd just get takeaway or something.'

'Takeaway!' Mum said. 'Do you really think that McDonald's and Pizza Hut came out with the First Fleet?'

Oh! I realised then that when she'd said 'you', she hadn't meant me, Dan Baker, but me the convict. (What was my name?)

'You can take some of the camping utensils if you like,' Mum went on. 'But make sure they come back, okay?'

'Okay.' But somehow the thought of it (the bush, the cooking-for-myself, the hard earth, the snakes) had gone sour, and I shoved the wire and stuff back on the shelf. I was me, Daniel John Baker, this was the last decade of the twentieth century, and I was a free person, so as the rain had stopped I went down to the milkbar where everyone hangs out. (Somehow I just had to see them. I mean, I knew I'd make new friends in Perth, but still ...)

It was a couple of nights later when I was watching TV (Mum was out at her photography course) that I suddenly thought 'Seamus'. The name just came into my head and I knew that was me. Seamus Murphy. That meant I was Irish, didn't it?

That was all at that stage, but it's funny how, when you become aware of something, it somehow seems to crop up all the time. Over the next week, there was a show on TV about all the fighting between the Irish people and the English landlords that's been going on for centuries, and in English we did a poem about the Easter Rebellion. And then Mum's friend Liz who's overseas sent this postcard of a tiny fallen-down stone cottage on a headland, with the sea on one side and steep green paddocks all around and a little village with a church spire in the distance.

That's *it*, that's where I come from, I just knew. I read the caption on the back of the postcard: *Deserted Cottage, Connemara, Ireland.*

The next day in library period I found myself looking up Connemara in the atlas, but it seemed to be a whole area. I ran my finger down the jagged coastline, reading the names of the villages — why didn't the bloody postcard say exactly where I lived? I shut my eyes and kept fingering the map, as if that might help me remember, and then I was aware of everyone laughing and the librarian saying, 'Daniel! Daniel! You look as if you're holding a seance!'

If this is all sounding as if I was getting totally obsessed with the history thing, then I'm giving the wrong impression. Most of the time I was just the same as ever (except for the uneasiness with Mum). I was going out skating with my mates after school, or playing computer games round at Damien's place. On Friday nights we usually went to Jason's (his parents run the video shop and he gets all the latest movies for free). One Saturday I went down to Penrith with Tim and mucked around, and twice I went to the disco at the Youth Centre. Meanwhile I'd rung Dad and told him I wanted to move over to Western Australia at the end of the year, and he said he knew, Mum had already rung him and discussed it. (That pissed me right off. Whose future was it anyway?)

'Okay, but leave it till January,' Dad said. 'I've got to come to Sydney — the band's doing a bit of a tour across to the east, finishing up on New Year's Eve at a pub in Rozelle. Then I guess I could drive up, we could pack your stuff in the Kombi, and you could come back to Perth with me. But there won't be much room,' he warned. 'I'll have a lot of the band equipment. So keep it down to a couple of bags, okay?'

'No worries,' I said. If you're used to living out of a shoebox (the Seamus bit of me thought) then a couple of bags sounds like heaps of room. All the same, I didn't find it easy when I started going through sixteen years of accumulated junk, making a big pile to take to the op shop.

Toy trucks and cars from when I was a real little kid; the bulldozer Dad gave me the Christmas after he split; Monopoly and Junior Scrabble and Uno and Chinese Chequers; the farm set (I used to really love that); Little Golden Books and *Thomas the Tank Engine* and the Hardy Boys and Paul Jennings and Roald Dahl; the plastic speedcar raceway and the Lego and my surfaplane. And then there were all the clothes I'd grown out of, and four brand new pairs of pyjamas (Nan gave me some every birthday and I never wore them).

The other pile was the hardest because I'd have to take it to the tip. Stuff like my three broken skatedecks and all my old Reeboks and Nikes that I'd worn out skating; my first football (that had punctured when Tim and I were playing near the highway and a car went over it); my first cricket bat (that had split down the middle when Damien hit a six right down the back gully and we never found the ball); the two-way radio (that Jason and I had made out of beer cans and clothesline); and Dino, my old green velvet dinosaur, who was sprouting fluff from his earholes. I just had to look at that stuff and I'd remember all the good times ...

'I never thought I'd see the day,' Mum stuck her head around the door, 'when Daniel Baker voluntarily cleaned his room!'

'I'm not cleaning. I'm throwing stuff out.'

'What in heaven's name for!'

'Well, you won't want all my junk,' I said, 'when you set up your darkroom.'

'Oh ...' I'd caught her out, I could see. She hadn't actually told me about her plans for when she got rid of me. 'Okay, but you don't have to pack *now*, do you? Dad won't be coming to get you till New Year. And we can't shift all that stuff, without a car.'

'Just practising,' I said. 'Making sure it'll fit when the time comes.' I looked at my third pile: *Things to Take*. My skateboard. Tapedeck. Tapes. My Swiss army knife. One pair of jeans (besides the pair I had on), two pairs Mambo shorts, four T-shirts, tracksuit pants, sweatshirt, coat. And the hardback set of *The Lord of the Rings* that Mum had given me when I'd started high school. That was Dan Baker's convict box.

'Oh by the way,' Mum said, real sort of off-hand. 'I saw this in the op shop and got it for you. I hope you don't mind.'

She held out something that looked like a tin whistle. What the hell could it be?

'It's a tin whistle,' Mum said. 'I thought it might cheer you up.'

I stared at her. Okay, throwing out all my stuff *was* making me miserable, but she didn't know that. And the last thing I needed was more junk.

'When you're by yourself at night. In your hut, if you have a hut.'

Oh. It was you-the-convict she meant again. 'Thank you,' I said rather stiffly. 'But I don't know if Seamus can play it.'

'Seamus?'

'Yeah, Seamus Murphy. That's me ...'

When I said that, I ... Look, I'm not trying to make this out to be like an SF movie or something. Nothing spooky happened, such as seeing my hand go all calloused and warty, or hearing moans, or the room going sideways, but I did feel — something. As if someone out in space had a machine like a TV remote control, and they'd flicked for a second from my channel to Seamus Murphy's channel and then back again.

'I mean,' I said quickly, 'that's *him*. The convict that I am.'

'That's appropriate,' Mum said.

'What is?'

'That you're Irish.'

I looked at her.

'Well you are,' Mum explained. 'On my side. Nan was a MacBride before she married. Not that she's ever been to Ireland or anything — we're about fifth generation Aussie. But still. Oh well, if you don't want this, I suppose I can give it back to the op shop ...'

'No, it's okay,' I said. 'Maybe I could learn to play it.'

'Maybe you could and all,' I heard Mum say in a put-on Irish voice from the other side of the door.

After that, it felt even more like I didn't really live here any more. The junk pile stayed (it's still here now); Mum never told me to clean it up, and it was as if I was just sort of camping in the room.

And so the month disappeared. If I still sometimes thought stuff like 'A bit of broken mirror — I could make fire with that!' or 'There's that rusty fishing knife in the garage ...', I was mostly thinking of my new life, the one I'd have in Perth. No school — I'd just hang out with Dad — travel round in the van to wherever he was playing. There'd be all these chicks at the gigs — I'd grow my hair and get a couple of earrings ... Maybe the band would take me on as a roadie; it was a pity I wasn't musical (I'd had a few goes at the whistle but it just made this high lonely noise, like the wind).

And then it was a Thursday afternoon, the assignment was due in the next day, and I didn't even have a shoebox, let alone all my convict belongings. Leave it till after tea, I thought, the garage had a light and I'd just grab some of the camping gear and some wire and bolts and stuff. Oh, and write a couple of letters. Ms Pap wanted some letters in the box, she said, to show the research we'd done. Ha ha.

It was 6.30, just on dark, and Mum was sitting down to watch *EastEnders* when the TV and light went off.

'Quick, Dan,' Mum said, 'nick out and get the fuse — here's the little torch — and I'll look for the fuse wire.'

But when I went out to the fuse box I realised that it wasn't just one of our fuses: the whole street was in darkness, not a light on anywhere, and as I looked out over the town I saw ... well I saw nothing, because it was completely black.

Now I should have said that there was a dreadful wind that evening — I could feel it tearing at me the minute I opened the door, and I could hear it rushing through the branches of the pine trees all around our house. It sounded like the surf, it was so loud and kind of pounding.

'Quick, come inside, Danny!' I heard Mum yelling through the kitchen window. 'A branch might fall!' Just then there was a great flash of lightning, and a boom of thunder.

I pelted back in, and by now of course Mum had realised what had happened. 'Thank Christ for Seamus,' she said. I thought she'd really flipped, and then she said, 'I thought you might be needing a bit of candle for your project, so I went to buy one, but they made me take a whole box. I know they're here somewhere, give us the torch ...'

The torch. It wasn't in my hand.

'Oh well,' Mum said, 'they are here somewhere.'

We stumbled around in total darkness, like a game of blind man's bluff. Suddenly the house was unfamiliar, and doorways, the dresser, a chair at an angle became things to crash into. I remember at one stage our feet hit something and we fell together in a pile. It was the first time we'd touched in ages. 'Bloody skateboard!' Mum said. Then down there, on the floor, with the storm crashing at the windows, we started laughing. 'On top of the fridge,' Mum finally said. 'That's where convicts keep their candles.'

We lit all six of them, three up each end of the kitchen table. The fuel stove was going, Mum was cooking one of her oxtail stews. Potatoes in the oven. We were warm, and wouldn't starve, but it really was a bit scary, not the thunder and lightning, but knowing that the pine trees were huge, and far too close to the house, and shallow rooted in the sandy soil, and the wind could easily bring one down. That's obviously what had happened to the electricity: trees had brought down the lines all over the town.

'Oh well,' I said, 'it'll be a good excuse to tell Ms Pap.'

'Come again?'

'Why I can't get my convict stuff together. Why I can't write my letters.'

She started then. What letters etc. etc.??? I told her and she went on to: 'Why do you always leave all your homework till the last night?' Then bit her lip. Since the bad blue, it was as if she really *had* decided that it was *my* homework, *my* School Certificate, *my* future.

'But you might as well,' she urged, 'write the wretched letters tonight. I mean, Ms Pap will just make you do it for Monday. And it's not as if there's any TV, or you can listen to music, or do anything else.'

When she said that, I thought: we're stuck together tonight. I can't disappear to my room and listen to tapes, she can't sit in the lounge and watch TV, we are together for a whole night with none of the toys of the twentieth century to help us not to talk to each other.

So that's how I started. In the dark kitchen, with the

THE CONVICT BOX

fuel stove going, the smell of stew, the crashing surf noise of the wind through the pines, the photograph flares of lightning through the window, the boom of the thunder, the flicker of the candlelight, me up one end of the kitchen table, and my mother up the other. And half a world between us.

> Mace's Farm
> Coxs River
> New South Wales
> 24 January 1832

To My Mother,
I hope you are feeling good. Though I have been in this country for more than a year, this is the first chance I have had to write to you, as up until now I didn't have a pencil.
I will tell you of the trip over here first. The boat we travelled on was very overcrowded. All of us were treated and fed very poorly, resulting in numerous deaths from scurvy and other causes.
Shortly after I arrived in Sydney Town I got into a fight with some of the other prisoners. I swear to you it wasn't my fault but when you are new in a place, people pick on you and test you out to see what you are made of. So this group of three men began to taunt me, laughing at the way I speak and saying Ireland is a boghole, and I began to argue back, and the next thing I know we are all fighting on the ground and an overseer arrives and the others say I started it. As a result I was sentenced to 12 months in an ironed gang and sent to

work on the new road at Victoria Pass. That was sheer Hell — working in leg irons, breaking rock, grubbing out massive tree roots, carting huge blocks of sandstone for the culverts. We rose at daybreak and worked all day, and at night slept in bark huts (5 or 6 men to a hut) inside a stockade.

Anyway, I do not wish to worry you, and that is over now. I have been assigned to a Master called Mr Mace and I arrived at his farm yesterday. The farm is out on the western plains, beyond the mountains, and I am told it is 650 acres of which 5 are cultivated. At the farmhouse, there are two other men in service (one of them kindly gave me this pencil) but I am to work alone as a shepherd at the other end of Mr Mace's land. I will finish now, as there seems little point writing when I do not know how I will ever post this to you. Your Son, Seamus Murphy.

Mace's Farm
Coxs River
New South Wales
17 April 1832

Dear Mother,

I hope you are well. It is three months now since last I wrote to you but there is little News, as one day here is very much the same as the next.

I have a little hut of bark and thatch, and my job is to keep an eye on the sheep by day and herd the flock into their pen at night in case the dingoes get them. It is easy work, compared to building the road, but boring and lonely, for my only companions are the sheep and the

THE CONVICT BOX

flies, the snakes and mosquitoes.

Once a week Mr Mace rides out to check up on me and bring me supplies. I am entitled to 1 pound of beef or mutton a day but he sometimes brings kangaroo instead. This meat is very rich and has a good taste, a bit like oxtail. The problem is that in the hot summer months the meat is flyblown within hours, so I subsist on damper-bread and fish that I catch in the nearby river.

So that is really all I can tell you of my life here, for nothing ever happens. Sometimes at night when I am in the hut I think of our cottage, by itself on the hillside. After Dad died, I guess you and I got used to the loneliness, but it's a different feeling, to be alone here. I write hoping that one day I might meet someone who can take my letters to you. As an assigned servant, I have no money, and just one small box of belongings. I play the tin whistle that you gave me, but as you know I have no musical Talent. Remember Dad, and how he would play his fiddle for all the dances!

Your loving Son, Seamus Murphy.

THE NIGHT TOLKIEN DIED

Mace's Farm
Coxs River
New South Wales
17 July 1832

Dear Ma,
Since I have come here I have realised how important it is to read and write and I am thankful that you forced me to go to Father Malarkey, and learn. Though I still do not know how I will ever send these letters to you, it is a comfort to me, just to write them.
Tonight there is a tremendous Storm, and I am afraid. I could not have said this to you, at home, but here sometimes things are frightening. Do you remember how the sea would crash against the cliffs, on our headland? Well, here sometimes it feels as if the very land is our enemy. And I feel like an alien in it. I wish you were here.
Love from Seamus.

'Here,' Mum said. We'd eaten the stew and spuds as I'd been writing, and she'd made a pot of coffee. 'A dash of the Irish,' she said. And blow me down if she didn't get out the bottle of whisky she'd won in the Volunteer Bushfire Brigade Christmas raffle and pour a slurp into each of our mugs. Now this was weird — Mum being against grog as she is — but what was even weirder was that she passed across a letter that seemed to be written exactly to me, Seamus.

THE CONVICT BOX

> c/- St Josephs Presbytery
> Ballyfermough
> Connemara
> 17 July 1832

My Dear Son,
Father Malarkey has kindly offered to write this letter for me, for as you know I have no schooling, and he says that if I send it care of H.M. Prisons it may reach you. It is some years now since you left, to go to the city, and then after your trouble, they took you far away, and though I have not heard from you since then and sometimes wonder if you are still alive, I just want you to know that I think of you and pray for you.

We are all struggling by here as usual. His Lordship has raised the rent again and the MacBrides have been evicted. Last winter was the worst I ever remember. I think of you there in the sun, and I know it seems wrong to say this, but at times I think we should all break the law and be transported, for no punishment could be worse than what we endure. Still, I should not dwell on our troubles, for I know that your time out there will not be easy, amongst the snakes and the heathens. And we hear tales of savage beatings, and I pray that you are safe.

Oh my Son, I was never able to talk to you when you were here, and now it is so hard, for I have to speak through miles of distance. And I know that you thought that I was a nag and a shrew, for I sent you to learn your letters, and I forced you and I pushed you, because I did not want you to be like me, and stuck in a place like this for ever. But while I harrassed you under my roof, I never told you that my heart would catch every time you walked in the door. So that I would hide my joy in you by picking on your faults, until one day you were gone. And now your Absence is a continual source of Grief to

Your Loving Mother.

So that was then, this is now. (That's the title of an S.E. Hinton novel that I got for Christmas, but it fits this just as well.)

31 December, and it's countdown to blast-off. I said at the beginning that I'm not always sure where the reality stops and the invention starts (how did Mum make up the same weird priest's name that I did?) and since that time I've sometimes felt kind of haunted, but in a good way, by this bloke I made up. I mean that since then, I've felt Seamus in me, known him as part of me. And through him I know that I can do it alone. Just me, and my piece of wire, my nails, my broken mirror, my tin whistle. Or me and a pair of Mambo shorts, my Swiss army knife, my tape deck, my skateboard.

At the same time, I know that because I can do it, I don't have to. Yet.

Like late that winter's night, after I'd gone to bed, I woke and the wind had stopped and the silence was thick around the house. I looked out the window, and the snow had started. I went to the back door, put my gumboots on, so I could go rushing out into it, like I used to do when I was a little kid. And then I looked at the snow that was starting to cover the ground in perfect newness, and I thought: it'll be even deeper if I leave it till the morning.

Now I say to Mum, 'Let's catch the train down to Sydney this arvo. We can go to Rozelle, see Dad play ...'

'Okay,' she says, 'but what about all your stuff?'

'I'm staying,' I say.

My mum isn't very good at showing what she's feeling so she just starts shifting the junk from the floor back into the shelves and cupboard. We work for a while together in silence but when I pick up my tape deck I accidentally press *Play,* and Jimi Hendrix blasts out.

Mum turns to me now with a look on her face as if 'Are You Experienced?' is the best thing she's ever heard.

'Welcome home, Seamus Murphy,' she says.

THE NIGHT TOLKIEN DIED

Lórien set the drinks on the tray as Noni poured them. The wine glasses at the dining table were heirlooms, Venetian crystal, but for drinks out on the terrace before lunch they just had the best modern Swedish (except for Vern of course, who got a small tumbler that had once held Vegemite). The tray was silver, with an inscription memorialising the twenty-five years that Grandfather had served as President of the golf club. Lórien had never met him. He had died of a heart attack at the nineteenth green (Noni always said) straight after being re-elected President, for the twenty-sixth time, at the 1973 Annual General Meeting. It was only recently that Lórien had realised that the nineteenth green was the clubhouse bar, and that her grandfather was a drunk, like Vern. She'd been born in 1974, a year too late for Grandfather, but in plenty of time for her own sixteenth birthday, which was the reason for today's luncheon party.

Noni named the intended recipient of each drink as she handed it to Lórien.

'*Me* ...' (Typical that she'd start with herself.) A long slim glass filled with tinkling ice and the sunrise blush of a campari and soda that matched Noni's raw silk shirt and set off the cornflower blue of her eyes, the silver-rose of her hair. Made curious by the colour of the drink, Lórien sneaked a sip while her grandmother turned back to the bar trolley. *Shudder.* It was like that mouthwash that Lórien had been prescribed when she'd had a strep throat. *Shudder again.* She couldn't get the taste out. And yet it had looked so enticing ...

'*The Colonel* ...' Noni went on. This time it was a brandy and dry, no ice, in a medium-sized glass with a heavy bottom. The Colonel was Noni's bridge partner, officially; unofficially, her lover. He'd been around for as long as Lórien could remember. A balding little gent with a small pot belly, who wore a fawn safari suit in summer and tweeds in winter.

'*Glad* ...' The driest of dry sherries. Glad was the Colonel's sister. Same pot-belly, but tweeds all year round. Lórien secretly rather liked her, but never knew what to say; she suspected the feeling was mutual.

'*For Win* ... *a Pimms* ...' How Noni could manage to express so much derision in four syllables, Lórien couldn't imagine. The Pimms, like Noni's own drink, was in a long ice-filled glass, but looked tawdry with its clutter of cucumber and mint and lemon. Win was Glad's partner at the *Green Thumb*, and lived with Glad and the Colonel in the old house at the back of the nursery; or rather, Glad and the Colonel lived with Win, for it was Win's skill at playing the stock exchange that had bought the property and the business, and that continued to support the three of them as plant sales slumped through the recession. Win's looks belied her brain, for she resembled a fluffy old pussy cat, and indeed seemed to moult hairpins and cardigans and lolly wrappers wherever she sat. Noni detested her — *not* (Noni insisted) because she was lesbian but because she was petit-bourgeois; that was Noni's least favourite class of people, Noni always said.

As if to rid her mind of Win, Noni made a great deal of clatter releasing a new tray of ice into the silver pitcher. Reaching for yet another tall glass she measured gin, added tonic, two cubes of ice, a twist of lemon. '*Mother* ...' she said as she handed it, meaning of course not her mother but her daughter, Lórien's mum, whom Noni always treated with a scrupulous formality. Lórien wondered as usual what it had been like to be Noni's child, but there was no time for speculation because Noni was already moving on to the next customer, about whom she made her feelings quite unambiguous.

'*Your father* ...' A frosty glass beer mug, and a can of a certain brand of Lite that Dad always reckoned was rat's piss.

'He asked for Coopers,' Lórien reminded her. Dad made home brew, and liked thick brown yeasty-flavoured beer.

'Nonsense,' Noni contradicted. 'He's driving.'

So was Mum, and so was Glad, but that hadn't worried Noni. Lórien of course didn't point this out.

As if to make up, Noni poured a hefty slug of Scotch into another glass, handed it straight, no water, no ice. '*Mitch* ...' she announced, this time rolling the name warmly on her tongue, even smiling as it came out. Why the difference? Lórien was, as always, puzzled. Mitch was Dad's best mate, had been since school; then they'd gone together to university, rented a house together, got arrested together in anti-Vietnam demonstrations, started a little magazine together, got drunk together, smoked dope together, whatever. But whereas Dad for years now had been pretty respectable — he was head of English at a selective high school, for heaven's sake — Mitch was still a bum. On the dole, except for when he very occasionally got a Literature Board grant; but that was it: he was a Poet. In Noni's view one might as well say Prince. ('One of the unacknowledged legislators of the world,' Dad himself always said when he came down in the morning to find Mitch snoring in the middle of the lounge room floor, where he'd collapsed; it was a sign of their friendship that Mitch still had a key to Dad's place and would sometimes turn up unannounced and off his face.) Of course Noni never actually *read* Mitch; it was enough to tell the solo girls that one of the guests at her luncheon party was a young man who had just been short-listed for the Premier's Prize. Mitch was present today in his capacity as Lórien's godfather: back when she had been born — illegitimately, to Noni's horror — Mum and Dad had tried to placate Noni about the absence of a wedding by providing a christening, complete with Mitch as godfather and Noni herself as godmother. It hadn't worked, as Noni's continuing coldness to Dad and coolness to Mum attested. But at least Mitch provided a distraction on social occasions, for when he was present Noni was too in awe of his reputation to bother overmuch with sniping at Dad ...

'Huh?' Lórien realised her grandmother was saying something.

'I said, *"This is for your uncle Vern,"*' Noni enunciated through gritted teeth. The small Vegemite glass (Vern's co-ordination wasn't good at times) was stacked to the brim with ice cubes, over which Noni now squirted the smallest possible splash of white from a cask. She shuddered, as Lórien had done at Noni's own drink, though whether at the degradation of Chateau Cardboard or at the degradation of her son's situation, was not clear. For if Mitch at forty was, in most people's eyes, under-employed and over-indulgent, there was no polite phrase for dear Vern.

A drunk, a desperate, a druggie, a deadbeat ... Vern was a piece of flotsam left behind when the tide of the sixties went out. Pencil thin, he still wore flared velvet jeans, and sandals made out of car tyres. His hair, though turning grey and receding from his brow, still dribbled down past his shoulders, and his dialogue — or at worst his monologue — was at times still larded with flower-power slang. In short, as Mum always said, dear Vern was a Living Treasure of the Age of Aquarius; the only trouble was, as Mum also said, dear Vern wouldn't be living much longer.

It was as part of the attempt to stop him from dying that Noni rationed his drinking down to this apology for alcohol that was hopefully just enough to stop his body from screaming out so badly that he would sneak in to get something stronger ...

'And now the teetotallers,' Noni concluded brightly. From the fridge door she selected not the Perrier but the

No Frills mineral water. Poured it. *'For what's-her-name ...'*

'Jocelyn,' Lórien reminded her, knowing full well that her grandmother knew the name of her stepmother. Knowing too that it had been the final straw for Noni when Dad had married his pregnant girlfriend a couple of months ago, given that he had neglected to marry a different pregnant girlfriend sixteen years before. Not that Mum had wanted to, of course; it was against her anarchist principles. But that made no difference to the way Noni would stare at Jocelyn's bulge, as if resentful that the foetus in there would come into the world with the proper paperwork, while her granddaughter was nothing better than a bastard ...

'And last but not least ...' Noni paused as if for a roll of drums. *'For the birthday girl herself...'*

(Gee wow thanks. A goblet of sparkling black Coca Cola. Lórien glanced at her watch. Only six hours or so till her real party would begin ...)

After eating was over and the washing up was stacked in the machine, the four older members of the party retired with tiny china coffee cups to the comfort of the lounge room for a rubber or two of bridge and a bit of a snooze, and the five middle-aged and one young adult member of the party took large pottery coffee mugs way down the end of the garden, where a cluster of deck chairs squatted beneath a camouflage of weeping willow.

'Out of sight out of mind,' Mitch said as they settled.

'Wow yeah, man,' Vern breathed. 'That was so heavy.'

'Cosmic,' agreed Mitch, who at times resuscitated sixties jargon to set Vern further down the time warp. 'Transcendental.'

'Mitch, stop it,' Mum snapped.

'Oh stop it yourself, Annie,' Mitch snapped back. 'I thought we'd just escaped from the bloody moralisers. Let him be. As John Lennon didn't quite say.'

Dad was doing mime signals at Mitch, meaning: would you like some beer in your coffee mug? The idea was that if Vern didn't think they were drinking, then he mightn't want to too. Fat chance. As they knew. But they went through the motions. At least at first.

'Yes please, mate,' Mitch mimed back.

Behind a willow frond, Dad poured Coopers into two mugs while Vern minded his own business by pulling the cask of white out of his patchwork shoulder bag, resting it on a log, and turning the tap full into *his* mug. 'Anyone else?' he politely offered the circle.

Jocelyn looked away, embarrassed. This was only her second family occasion; the first had been the wedding, at which Vern had passed out in the restaurant's soup.

Mum virtuously sipped at her mug, which had real coffee in it; and also real whisky — just a dash to help her get over the tension of lunch.

Dad let out a snort of laughter, at the hypocrisy of himself, the whole situation. 'No thanks, mate,' he told Vern. 'I'll stick with this.' He plunked the beer bottle out in the open.

Vern didn't even see. He was well beyond noticing what other people did. All there was was his body, which needed alcohol, as other people's bodies needed air, food, water, sex, other things. Mum had tried to explain to Lórien. It wasn't any longer a matter of *wanting* to drink — like choosing — deciding. His body chose for him, and if he didn't do it, his body rebelled by shaking, sweating, screaming, throwing fits ...

Of course, there were ways around it. Or half-ways. Places you could go to, to dry out. Get off it. Problem was, Vern always got on it again.

Whose problem?

Why Vern?

Change the subject.

It's my birthday, Lórien thinks, and I'll have a good time if I want to. Only three and a half hours now, and I'll be able to go to Beccy's place. Meanwhile sit here, beneath the willows, watching the adults, as I've been watching them (except for Jocelyn, who is new on the scene) since I was born ...

Now Mitch beside me takes out a bag of dope, rolls a joint, lights it. So what's new?

Ah, this is: he offers it towards the left, to me.

What to do?

Multiple Choice time:

- ☐ Yes ☐ No
- ☐ True ☐ False
- ☐ Will she? ☐ Won't she?

As usual, any chance that I might answer the question myself is taken out of my hands.

'*Mitch!*' protests my mother. 'She is exactly sixteen!'

'*Annie!*' protests my godfather. 'That is exactly the reason I am offering it to her!'

'Now I am sixteen,' I chip in, 'I have custody over my own body.' I try to say it lightly, like a joke, but it goes down like a saucepan of cold porridge.

'*See!*' Mum yells at Mitch. 'See what you've started now! It's all very well for you to keep your bloody anarchist principles intact. You don't have a teenage daughter!'

Mitch doesn't reply, takes a deep lungful of smoke, and as he holds it in he offers the joint to the right, to Mum.

Mum shakes her head in a high and mighty way as if

THE NIGHT TOLKIEN DIED

to suggest that Mitch should know by now that she is a total abstainer from illegal substances.

Mitch offers it to the person on Mum's right: Jocelyn. The same Jocelyn who had mineral water at lunch and brought her own camomile teabags for when others might indulge in caffeine. The very Jocelyn who pats her bulge now in a self-important way and smiles: No thanks. Baby on board.

Mitch reaches out across the circle to Dad who is opposite him. Dad smiles wryly, shoots a nervous glance at Jocelyn, then takes the joint in a way that is meant to look as if he is just being polite and doesn't want to hurt Mitch's feelings. After one drag, he offers it to his right, to Vern.

Now Mum turns on Dad. *'Robert!'* Protecting not her young daughter any more, but her elder brother.

'Honestly, Annie,' Mitch says, 'it'd harm him a bloody sight less than that rotgut wine he keeps ladling into his bloodstream.'

Vern takes the joint, but only in the way that he might politely have accepted anything offered him, just to be allowed to drink in peace. He holds it for a while as he sips, then puffs at it as if it is an ordinary cigarette, then puts it down to burn on the edge of the log as he squirts a top-up into his drink. He forgets of course to pick it up again.

Mitch rescues the joint, hands it again towards Mum (who this time absentmindedly accepts it), and resumes the argument about me. 'Just as it seems to me preferable for Lórien to smoke *this* stuff, which a mate of mine grew and I know to be decent,' Mitch says, 'than to run off and spend her pocket money buying impure bloody acid that's full of strychnine and crap!'

Blush. That's what Beccy's getting me for my birthday. Well, not impure crap or anything, but acid. She reckons it's really good. She's tried it heaps of times. Well, twice. Her parents are away tonight. There'll just be the two of us there. Oh, and maybe a couple of guys Beccy knows. I've never tried acid before. I can't wait.

And so the afternoon settled in beneath the willows as the green fronds made a shield to keep the world out, and the talking — such as it was — seemed to stretch in long thin strands from grown-up to grown-up, around and across the circle, like the first pattern-making of a spider's new web.

Despite the anticipation of her real party, Lórien was content, for she always found that her mind could drift most freely when the adults engaged in this sort of desultory dope-talk. She'd once gone with Dad on a holiday to Thailand, and she'd found the same thing there: sitting by herself at an outdoor market restaurant, surrounded by the clamour of a language that she couldn't understand at all, she found that her exclusion brought a curious peace. It was the same now.

As the conversation passed around movies she hadn't seen and books she hadn't read, she felt her mind filling with a pleasant languor. Vern too was silent, dwelling somewhere inside his mind — or wine. Then, as the other four adults spun backwards and forwards the titles of the current ideologically acceptable novels, Vern leaned towards Lórien, as if seeking to include her, and ernestly confided, 'You know, the only thing I have been able to read for quite some time now is *The Lord of the Rings'.*

Lórien was not quite sure what to say to a grown person who was somehow stuck in the same mindset as her contemporaries: for the trilogy was the cult book of Beccy's gang and indeed, last year, before Lórien had been admitted to the group, they had even gone on a two-day hike, wearing green cloaks and taking only hobbit food and marijuana.

Vern coughed and continued, and his voice came out loudly, as if he was making an important announcement. 'Yes, I still love Tolkien,' Vern said. 'Just as much as ever.'

Silence shattered the web-making. For a moment, Lórien thought it was simply because Vern had spoken.

But then she saw the looks passing between Mum and Dad, Dad and Mitch, Mitch and Mum — and the daggers-look on Jocelyn's face, as she too observed what Lórien saw. And then — wonder of wonders — Vern's face for a moment clicked out of his wine haze and Lórien knew that these four who had once shared a house now shared a memory so strong that you could almost see the bonds ...

Until Jocelyn's bright voice broke through: 'So when did the rest of you grow out of *Lord of the Rings?*'

Lórien knew that Jocelyn's question had been intended merely to get everyone chatting again, change the subject; however, not only did the silence deepen, but Mum, Dad and Mitch looked alarmed, as if some guilty secret had been touched upon.

At last Mitch answered: 'It was the night Tolkien died ...'

'What was?' Lórien jumped in.

Mitch didn't answer her directly, but glanced at Mum and Dad. 'You know,' he said to them, 'since that night, I haven't even been able to look at the cover of it.'

Mum and Dad seemed to be squirming in their deck chairs.

'*Why — what happened?*' Lórien demanded.

'*Nothing,*' Mum said quickly — far too quickly. '*Nothing.* Just one night in — 1973, it must have been —

when we four were sharing a house, we heard on the television news that J.R.R. Tolkien had died, that's all.'

For some reason, Lórien remembered the silver tray. '1973,' she said. 'That's when Grandfather died too.'

'That's right!' Mum seized the chance to move into general reminiscence. 'It was after Dad died in August 1973 that I was able to move out of home to live with Mitch —'

Oops! Mum caught herself.

'With *Mitch!* You were living with *Mitch?*'

Lórien's mother was bright red now, ripping leaves off a handy willow stem. Lórien's godfather was making a business of lighting a cigarette. Lórien's father was checking that his pregnant wife had enough pillows behind her ...

'So when did you start living with Dad?' Lórien did some quick mental arithmetic. It didn't allow much leeway: she was born in June 1974, so she must have been conceived in September the previous year.

Once again, Vern connected dangerously with the conversation. 'That was the night,' he explained, 'the night Tolkien died. At the beginning of it, she was on with Mitch. But by the time it finally ended, she was with Rob.'

'I think,' Jocelyn murmured, rising clumsily, 'I might just go up to the house and make myself a camomile tea ...'

Vern went on, as if proud that for once he was able to remember the same bit of the past that the others were thinking about. 'See, I'd had this acid in the fridge for a while,' he told Lórien, 'waiting for an occasion, so when we heard the bad news about Tolkien I brought it out ...'

'*Vern!*' Mum said sternly, shooting significant glances: Not In Front Of Lórien. But Vern of course was oblivious.

'And we all had some. I don't know if it was shit to start with, or if it'd gone off or something, but man, was that one bad trip ... Anyone else?' he concluded, turning the cask tap into his mug again.

'*Those orcs,*' Mitch said, as if in spite of himself he couldn't stop the words from coming out. 'I'll never forget those orcs. I went out into the backyard, to have a piss, and they were coming over the fence fast and furious ...'

'And the Nazgûl,' Dad cut in, as if he too had to verbalise the memory. 'Don't forget the Nazgûl.'

'I don't think I had the Nazgûl,' Mitch murmured.

'It just swooped down the corridor,' Dad went on. 'I felt its wings beating over me, this huge warm black flapping, that flapped on and on and ...'

'*Rob, stop it!*' Mum pleaded, but then she started too, for the conversation spider now was whizzing back and forth, across and round, in ever faster, tighter circles.

'And the chill,' Mum said, 'of the Barrow-wight, I can remember that chill, it went right through my bones, and there was a taste with it too, like biting on aluminium foil ...'

'And the smell,' Dad agreed, 'or maybe that was the Balrog, that smelled as if a septic tank had backed up.'

'What I remember,' Mitch chipped in, 'is the Dead Marshes. The carpet in the lounge room turned to black mud and reeds and I was trapped in it, and couldn't move my feet, and I was sinking.'

'And the howling of the wolves,' Mum said. 'I can hear that still. Howling and howling through the bathroom window.'

And so the catalogue went on, and Lórien listened, and she could see the horror reliving on the faces of her parents and her godfather as they told her of that night, but she knew that they had been protecting her and only telling her the nice bits when her uncle drifted back into the web and named the terror that had really held them all:

'*And the face of Sauron of Mordor on the kitchen wall!*'

The stillness was broken eventually by the sound of a brass gong reverberating down the long garden.

'*Lór-ien* ...' Noni's voice fluted from the terrace. '*Cake time* ...' It was the ritual at Noni's birthday luncheon parties that the cake ceremony took place at afternoon tea.

The willow group did not respond for a minute or two, for the reliving of the night Tolkien died had not yet settled into catharsis, but Glad's voice began to echo down in a bushman's *'Cooee! Cooee!'* and finally Dad said, 'C'mon, Vern mate, let's get you up to the house, eh?'

On the terrace was a series of white concentric circles. The round table, made of white wrought iron with a glass top, had been covered with a white linen cloth. Around this there crowded ten white wrought-iron chairs, and at each setting there was a white bread-and-butter plate and a dainty little white napkin with a hand-crocheted edge. At the centre of the table was a heavy silver plate, bearing a large round fruit cake with thick white marzipan icing and a ring of slender white candles. The only splash of colour was the pink writing that made another circle inside the candle ring, declaring: *'Happy Birthday Sweet Sixteen'*. At the heart of this, inscribed in silver, was the word *'LORIEN'*.

'Here,' said Noni, indicating a place near the French doors that led back into the lounge room. 'Birthday Girl at the top of the table.'

She sat herself at Lórien's right hand, conveniently near the teak traymobile on which the cups and saucers were gathered on the top shelf together with the silver teapot, the silver hot water jug, the silver milk jug and silver sugar bowl; on the lower shelf was a plate of club sandwiches, a plate of butterfly cakes, and a plate of Glad's cheese-and-cayenne wafers.

On Noni's right there now sat the Colonel, and on his right Jocelyn carefully squashed herself and bulge into the small space that cramped even further when Win chose the chair at Jocelyn's right.

Mitch grabbed the next one, which placed him in a straight line across the circle from Lórien. What if, she wondered, what if the swap that happened on that night hadn't happened? Then Mitch would be my father. A feeling of distaste ran through Lórien. Mitch was great fun as a godfather — indeed, when she'd been young he had been by far her favourite babysitter — but the thought of living with him on any regular basis ... She'd been to the place he rented: it was like a set from *The Young Ones*.

As Mitch settled himself now, Glad — who had clearly been intending to sit next to Win but had been pipped at the post — took the next seat.

Dad, who was half-carrying Vern, tried to plunk down beside Glad with Vern on his other side, thus leaving the chair on Lórien's left for Mum.

But at the crucial moment Vern lurched, Mum swerved back to avoid being knocked through the

French doors, Dad pushed Vern into the nearest chair, and once again Lórien found her uncle sitting on her left side.

Jocelyn glowered across the table as Mum took the only available seat, next to Dad.

'Lovely!' Noni lied. 'Well, now that everyone's comfortable, I'll start pouring ...'

If Noni had simply allowed Vern to keep sipping wine from his coffee mug, the disaster probably wouldn't have happened. But she insisted on exchanging the drink he'd brought up from the willows for a cup of tea, and then she dragged out the whole procedure of pouring and passing, of chatting and conversing, so that it was nearly an hour before she clapped her hands for attention, and after an hour without alcohol Vern was really starting to lose control.

'Matches,' Noni commanded, and the Colonel lit the candles.

A ragged chorus started up: *'Happy birthday to you/ Happy birthday to you/ Happy birthday dear L-o-r-i-e-n ...'*

Lórien blew the candles out.

'Happy birthday to you!'

The Colonel tried to follow this up with a round of *Why Was She Born So Beautiful?* but Noni silenced him with a look. 'Now remember to make a wish, sweetie!' And she thrust out a long sharp knife.

Perhaps it was the suddenness of her movement, or perhaps the knife connected with some dark dream remembered from the conversation beneath the willows, but as Lórien went to accept the knife Vern rose out of his chair, and — as if to protect Lórien — he grabbed the knife away from his mother. For a moment he stood, poised, holding the knife high. And then he lost balance, clawed with one hand at the air while the other hand pushed out and down, plunging the knife through Lórien's silver name.

As Vern's weight, slight though it was, fell full upon the centre of the circle, there was a horrendous crash and the cake on its heavy silver plate smashed straight through the glass-topped table, taking cloth, club sandwiches, cheesy wafers, teacups and saucers and all.

The most extraordinary aspect of the whole event was that Vern now simply sat down again, apparently oblivious of what had happened. As the other adults gasped and shrieked and made sure that their feet and legs hadn't been cut by the falling debris, Vern turned to Lórien and quietly confided, 'You know, the only book I've been able to read lately is *The Lord of the Rings*.'

THE NIGHT TOLKIEN DIED

In the car, heading up the highway, Lórien started to shiver.

'I'm so sorry, darling,' Mum said.

Shock changed to anger. 'What for, in particular?'

'Well,' Mum answered reasonably. 'Which particular piece of the catastrophe would you *like* me to be sorry for?'

Lórien shrugged. She didn't mind at all about Vern and the cake. It was the other bit. About the night Tolkien died.

As if she could read her daughter's mind, Mum said, 'Well, one good thing came out of that, anyway.'

'What?' Lórien demanded.

Mum said, 'You.'

They were nearly at Beccy's place when Mum added, 'Do you know why, out of all the names in Tolkien, your dad and I chose "Lórien" for you?'

Lórien shook her head.

'Because when the evil of Sauron of Mordor stretched over the whole of Middle Earth,' Mum said very softly, 'it was on the land of Lórien alone that no shadow lay.'

Lórien smiled back at her. That didn't make it completely better, but at sixteen you know that your mother can't make the past *un*-happen.

'Another thing,' Mum added formally, 'that I would like you to know is that, if that was the night when three of us lost the ability to love Tolkien, it was also the last time that any of us took acid.'

'Even Vern?'

'Especially Vern.'

'Mum,' Lórien suddenly found herself asking. 'What happened to Vern?'

'That night was just the climax,' Mum said. 'Acid, speed, grog, dope — Vern was right into whatever was going. He simply blew his mind, in the same way that you can blow an electrical circuit by overloading the power points. From that time on, he's been a walking and talking shell. Of course, for the last ten years or so it's been alcohol ...'

'How come?'

'Grog's cheap. Grog's legal. You don't need heroin to kill yourself, you know.' Mum's voice was breaking as she spoke of her brother, but Lórien wouldn't let the chance go.

'But why Vern?' Meaning: out of the four of you?

'I don't know,' Mum said as she double parked in front of Beccy's place. 'It's like Russian roulette.' She kept the engine running. 'You sure you don't just want to come home and have a quiet night? We could hire a video? Order a pizza?'

'No, it's okay ...'

THE NIGHT TOLKIEN DIED

It's my birthday, Lórien thinks as she runs up the path to Beccy's house, and I'll have a good time if I want to.

The bell chimes.

The door opens.

Beccy kisses me and hands me an envelope. Inside that is a card. And inside that is a small piece of blotting paper. And inside *that*...

What to do?

It's Multiple Choice time:

- ☐ Yes   ☐ No
- ☐ True   ☐ False
- ☐ Will she?   ☐ Won't she?